THAKAZHI SIVASANKARA PILLAI was born on 17 April 1912 in the village of Thakazhi in Alleppey District in the south-west Indian state of Kerala, where Malayalam is the language of 95 per cent of the population, though English is widely understood among the more highly educated. Thakazhi himself (for it is by the name of his village that he is normally known) went to the English-medium school in the nearby town of Ambalapuzha for his secondary education. In 1931 he went to Trivandrum to follow the pleadership course at the Law College, and he practised this profession until 1957.

The first of Thakazhi's forty novels, *Tyagatinnu pratiphalam* ('Reward for Sacrifice'), appeared in 1934, the year of his marriage to Kamalakshmi Amma. His best-known work outside Kerala is undoubtedly *Chemmeen* ('Shrimps', 1956), for it is the most widely translated, including the English version by Narayana Menon published in London and New York in 1962. His most ambitious work is the saga *Kayar* ('Coir' 1978). For *Enipadikal* ('Rungs of the Ladder', 1964; English translation, New Delhi 1976) he received the annual award of the Kerala Sahitya Akademi. Thakazhi is a Fellow of the Sahitya Akademi of India and has twice been President of the Kerala Sahitya Akademi. His distinction as a novelist and short story writer has been recognised by a number of other national and state awards.

R. E. ASHER is Vice-Principal and Professor of Linguistics at the University of Edinburgh. Among his publications in 1993 are *National Myths in Renaissance France* (Edinburgh University Press), and *The Encyclopedia of Language and Linguistics* in ten volumes (Pergamon) of which he is Editor-in-Chief. In 1982 he was elected a Fellow of the Kerala Sahitya Akademi and was awarded the Akademi's gold medal for services rendered to Malayalam language and literature. He is a Fellow of the Royal Society of Edinburgh and holds a PhD from the University of London and a DLitt from the University of Edinburgh. He has been a close friend of Thakazhi for thirty years.

THAKAZHI SIVASANKARA PILLAI

SCAVENGER'S SON (TOTTIYUTE MAKAN)

Translated from the Malayalam by
R. E. Asher

Do Not Trim Pages

HEINEMANN

Heinemann Educational
A Division of Heinemann Publishers (Oxford) Ltd
Halley Court, Jordan Hill, Oxford OX2 8EJ

Heinemann: A Division of Reed Publishing (USA) Inc.
361 Hanover Street, Portsmouth, NH 03801-3912, USA

Heinemann Educational Books (Nigeria) Ltd
PMB 5205, Ibadan
Heinemann Educational Boleswa
PO Box 10103, Village Post Office, Gaborone, Botswana

FLORENCE   PRAGUE   PARIS   MADRID
ATHENS   MELBOURNE   JOHANNESBURG
AUCKLAND   SINGAPORE   TOKYO
CHICAGO   SAO PAULO

First published in Malayalam in 1948 by
The Mangalodayam (Private) Ltd, Trichur
© Thakazhi Sivasankara Pillai 1948
This translation © R. E. Asher 1993
First published by Heinemann Educational in 1993

Series Editor: Ranjana Sidhanta Ash

British Library Cataloguing in Publication Data
A catalogue record for this book is available from the British Library.

Cover design by Touchpaper
Cover illustration by Ian Whadcock

ISBN 0435 950 827

Phototypeset by Wilmaset Ltd, Birkenhead Wirral
Printed and bound in Great Britain
by Cox & Wyman Ltd, Reading, Berkshire

93 94 10 9 8 7 6 5 4 3 2 1

CONTENTS

Introduction to the Asian Writers Series

Heinemann's new Asian Writers Series, aided by the Arts
Council of Great Britain, intends to introduce English language
readers to some of the interesting fiction written in languages
that most will neither know nor study.

For too long popular acclaim for Asian writing in the West
has been confined to the handful of authors who choose to write
in English rather than in the language of their own cultures.
Heinemann's entry into the field should dispel this narrow
perspective and place modern Asian writing within the broad
spectrum of contemporary world literature.

The first six works selected for the series are translations of
novels from five languages: Bengali, Hindi, Malayalam, Tamil
and Urdu. The six novels span seventy-five years of change in
the subcontinent. *Quartet*, one of Rabindranath Tagore's most
skilfully constructed and lively classics, was first published in
1916, whereas the most recent work chosen, *The Fire Sacrifice*,
was written by the up-and-coming Hindi novelist Susham Bedi
and first published in 1989.

These first six titles face the normal problems affecting
literature in translation, not least the difficulty of establishing
an exact parallel of the thought or verbal utterance of the
original in the target language. When the source text is in a
non-European language and embodies a culture and literary
style quite alien to English language readers, the translator's
task is made even more difficult.

Susan Bassnett in her invaluable work on translation studies
describes the typical colonial attitude to the literature of the

colonised as a 'master and servant' relationship, with the European translator attempting to 'improve' and 'civilise' the source text. At the other end of the scale she describes a kind of 'cannibalism' in which the translator almost 'devours' the text to disgorge a totally new product. Fortunately, the translators of this series fall into neither category but manage to retain a balanced view of their craft.

While it is very important to produce a translation that uses a style both readable and engaging to an English language readership, it must not obscure the particularities of literary devices, figures of speech, and aesthetic detail that the author uses to convey his or her sensibility, imagination and verbal artistry. Should such faithfulness to the original produce in the English version a greater degree of sentiment or charged imagery than the reader might expect, one hopes that he or she will be ready to accept the novelty of writing from an unfamiliar source.

In publishing the Asian Writers Series, Heinemann is taking a bold step into an area which has been neglected for too long. It is our hope that readers will respond with interest and enthusiasm as they discover the outstanding quality of these novels.

RANJANA SIDHANTA ASH, SERIES EDITOR, 1993

Introduction to Scavenger's Son

All the regions of India have their own individual charm. For those who have succumbed to the multi-faceted attractiveness of Kerala, it is difficult to imagine that any other part could be more seductive than this state in the southwest of the Republic, with its unparalleled natural beauty, its vigorous artistic and literary scene, and its passionate politics. Kerala's uniqueness partly derives from its mixture of religious communities – with Hindus, Muslims and Christians all making a significant contribution to its culture – and its exceptionally high level of literacy among both men and women. Linguistically it is the most homogenous of Indian states, with 95 per cent of its population being speakers of Malayalam, one of the four major Dravidian languages.

It is in this part of the country that Thakazhi Sivasankara Pillai was born in April 1912. His early notion that his destiny was that of a poet hardly outlived his adolescence and it is as a writer of prose fiction that he has made his name. The first of his short stories was published in 1929 and an estimated five hundred have followed. There are also forty novels, a play, a couple of volumes of autobiography, and a book about a visit he made to America, making Thakazhi a fairly prolific writer. Nevertheless his books are not produced quickly. A mentally planted seed sometimes takes many years to germinate and in this way the composition of his major novels overlaps, with one being developed in his mind while others which have been conceived earlier are being committed to paper. Thus he discussed with friends an idea for what was to become his most ambitious and perhaps his greatest novel some twenty years before it was published in 1978. This was *Coir*, a saga running to more than a thousand pages and telling the story of the life of a village over several generations. A decade later it became the basis for a successful television serial.

In common with many of his novels and stories, Thakazhi's *Coir* is set in the region of Kerala known as Kuttanad, of which the main town is Alleppey, the setting for *Scavenger's Son*. Kuttanad was known as the rice bowl of Kerala and farming was and is a major occupation. A good proportion of the fields are on land reclaimed from the backwaters. In earlier periods flooding was a constant hazard and life was generally hard. Much of what Thakazhi writes can be seen as an attempt to chronicle the effect of the nature of the land and of social conditions on the behaviour of the inhabitants. In particular he is concerned with the effect of change, including in more recent times the socio-economic impact of workers returning from relatively highly paid employment in the Gulf states.

It is not easy to identify the point at which Thakazhi attained maturity as a writer, for his technique as a novelist has continued to develop in interesting ways throughout his long life. He himself often talks of the contribution to his narrative art made in his childhood by his father's telling of the puranic tales which form the basis for kathakali, the traditional dance drama of Kerala, in which his father, Sankara Kurup, was a trained actor. However, the direction his writing took owes most to the time he spent in Trivandrum as a law student. There he met one of the most influential figures in twentieth-century Malayalam literature, A. Balakrishna Pillai, the radical editor of the journal *Kesari*. From him Thakazhi learnt not only about the great European novelists of the nineteenth century, particularly those of Russia and France, but also about the ideas of such figures as Freud and Bertrand Russell. It was during his student days that the progressive literature movement began to spread throughout India, and Thakazhi was much caught up in this.

The complex development and somewhat fugal nature of Thakazhi's published work does not allow an easy classification into a literary historian's periods, but three such stages have been identified. The first includes narratives which at the time they were published were widely regarded as sensational, on the grounds that they described patterns of sexual behaviour. The second includes novels and short stories which directly or indirectly express a political point of view, for example, *Scavenger's Son*, which was first published in 1947. Thirdly, there is the period in which Thakazhi has focused on a more subtle examination of the nature of interpersonal relationships. It is to this period that *Coir* belongs, as does the book for which Thakazhi is best known outside India, *Chemmeen* ('Shrimps', 1956), a tragic love story set among the fisher community of the coastal region to the south of Alleppey.

Although the word 'revolution' occurs a number of times in the final part of the book – in what is perhaps more of an epilogue than the last chapter of the story – *Scavenger's Son* may not, almost half a century after its publication, seem especially revolutionary. It is therefore important to approach it with some sense of historical perspective, remembering the social conditions which lay behind the anger of some of the characters in the novel and of the author himself. The leading figures in the narrative belong to a group which experiences the worst of these conditions, for they are outcastes, untouchables. Thakazhi does not talk directly about the evils of the caste system at a time when, unlike the present, the forms of discrimination lying at its heart were not outside the law. Even so, the development of the story shows what represents normality: namely the assumed impossibility of anyone born into the scavenger/sweeper class ever moving out of it to take on another occupation, however humble. A number of episodes also serve to remind the reader that a member of this class, even if scrupulously clean, remains 'unclean'.

In reading *Scavenger's Son* it is necessary, too, to bear in mind that the Malayalam novel, whose history did not begin until the late 1880s, had until Thakazhi's time been peopled with characters from the middle and upper levels of society. A novel which attempted to portray members of the very lowest stratum of society as if they were people capable of real human feelings was a very new departure.

Much has been written, in both Malayalam and English, about Thakazhi as a writer. The best single account is to be found in K. Ayappa Paniker's *Thakazhi Sivasankara Pillai* (Trivandrum, University of Kerala, 1988).

R. E. ASHER, EDINBURGH, 1993

Death

That night Ishukkumuttu did not sleep a wink. He had a first-class fever and cough. When day broke, his whole body ached. So he sent his son Chudalamuttu to see the overseer and let him know that he would have to take two days' leave.

When Chudalamuttu returned and gave an account of what had happened when he met the overseer, Ishukkumuttu could not believe what he heard. Ishukkumuttu had been working as a scavenger in the Alleppey municipality for thirty years. During this time the leave he had taken amounted to six or seven days. Yet when he asked to be given two days off the reply was that he would be replaced! And this was in spite of the fact that each month at least one-third of his wages had gone to the overseer.

'Did he really say he would replace me?' Ishukkumuttu asked his son.

'He said they've got someone for the job,' replied Chudala-muttu.

'Are they going to take him on this very day?'

'That's what he said.'

For a while Ishukkumuttu was silent. If somebody else was taken on to do his work what was he to do when he recovered from his illness? It had been his intention to hand over his scavenger's tin and shovel before he died. He had told a succession of overseers that, when he was no longer able to work, his son should be taken on in his place. Ishukkumuttu had done everything he possibly could to give satisfaction to all of them.

'Did you ask him to take you on?' he asked.

'No.'

Ishukkumuttu completely lost his temper. Picking up a stick that was lying nearby, he raised his arm. Chudalamuttu kept clear and the stick did not touch him. Ishukkumuttu began to cough. He then heaped abuse on Chudalamuttu. Chudalamuttu never does as he should. He is disobedient. He did not put the matter to the overseer as he should have done. If he had said that he himself should replace Ishukkumuttu, he would straight away have been taken on. The father concluded, 'You're useless! You didn't go in a serious frame of mind. He didn't like it.'

To think that another man would go into the latrines that he had cleaned out over a period of thirty years! It was too much for the old man. Why had he got the householders to make good the defects in the latrines? For his son's sake. To make his work easy.

In the late afternoon Ishukkumuttu took his stick and went out. Knotted in the end of the cloth he wore over his shoulders was a rupee and a half. Sitting, crawling, walking by turns, he got back when it was already quite dark. He called his son. Chudalamuttu would start the very next morning. But he would draw no pay for one month.

That night Chudalamuttu could not sleep. He too was going to become a scavenger. On two occasions he had worked as a sweeper to replace someone. Even then he had known that one day he would become a scavenger. That day was going to dawn. From now on he must live his whole life with tin and shovel.

He had already decided how he must live if he became a scavenger. He would not drink toddy. In the past many had invited him, but he had not had a drink. Nor would he in the future. Cannot a scavenger live like a human being? Cannot he too get some money together? With many such thoughts Chudalamuttu lay there.

An hour or two before daybreak Ishukkumuttu called Chudalamuttu. He explained the particular features of each house and gave him detailed instructions: one must be obedient; one must be tidy. Chudalamuttu agreed to follow these precepts. Choking, his eyes filled with tears, Ishukkumuttu gave his son his blessing.

'God will take care of my son. It is a father's tin and shovel that I am giving. By that means my son must live.'

The old man embraced his son and kissed him on the forehead. His eyes were full of tears. Bearing the blessing of a father's overflowing heart, Chudalamuttu went out. When he picked up the tin and shovel the old man called to him: 'My boy, there's a pot in that corner. Take that too. Only if you bring a little water shall I have anything to drink. Have you drunk anything?'

Chudalamuttu said nothing. Hearing his footsteps as he went, the old man asked again, 'Did you take it?' There was no reply from Chudalamuttu. Ishukkumuttu folded his hands in prayer: 'O God, grant that my son has rice to eat each day!'

So it was that on that day a young scavenger went to work in the Chandanakkow Ward, Alleppey.

Chudalamuttu's ward started at a road junction. At the junction was a hotel. Ishukkumuttu had instructed him to begin work there. When Chudalamuttu came out again from the latrine section of the hotel one of the waiters came with a couple of *doshas* and called to him: 'Under the eaves of that bathroom you'll find a small tin. Bring it and I'll give you some coffee.'

Chudalamuttu walked on without replying. The waiter shouted, 'Hey, you! It's you I'm calling.'

Chudalamuttu stopped, turned round and said, 'I don't want any.'

That seemed a remarkable thing to the hotel worker. He went inside. A little later the manager came down and went to the latrine. When he came out he said, 'Anyway, he's done a good job on the latrines.'

Chudalamuttu's refusal to accept the *dosha* and coffee was something quite out of the ordinary. The new scavenger was the main topic of conversation for some time. So people heard about the new scavenger and passed on the news.

The work to be finished by ten o'clock was the work of two days, and it had to be done properly. Before leaving to do it he had come across the overseer twice, and twice the latter had warned him that if he did not do the work properly he would be out of a job.

It was about eleven o'clock. Chudalamuttu would not be able to finish the work. He was very tired and he had had nothing to eat. At several houses he could have had rice left over from the previous evening. It seemed as if they were all under a compulsion to make him eat something. Because of that his obstinacy increased and he resolved not to take anything.

He did not want anyone's coffee or rice. If he could drink a mouthful of fresh water that would do. By the roadside a girl was taking water from a standpipe. Because of his thirst and weariness he asked without thinking, 'Would you run a little water into my mouth?'

Pinching her nose with thumb and finger, the child ran off.

Only at twelve o'clock was Chudalamuttu's work completed. The drum on his cart was full to the brim. Pushing it to the night-soil depot was another big job. The contents kept overflowing and falling on the road. Every so often he had to stop and sweep it up.

Chudala reached home dead tired. The old man inside was coughing – a cough to tear his body apart! Chudala shuddered. He was facing reality! Ishukkumuttu had had nothing to eat that day. He was lying there waiting for his son's arrival. Hearing the sound of footsteps outside, the old man called out, 'My boy, Chudala!'

Chudalamuttu was afraid to answer.

'Did you bring anything? My throat's parched.'

Chudala did not go in. Lying there, the old man asked, 'Did you have anything to eat?'

Not a sound!

Chudalamuttu couldn't stay. He felt as if he was standing on burning embers. Ishukkumuttu was crawling towards the door.

'Did the learned judge ask where I was? Did you tell the clerk your father was lying ill in bed?'

Chudalamuttu had disappeared. Ishukkumuttu came to the door and looked. There was no one to be seen. 'Didn't you come back? Oh God! Don't you know your father's tongue is parched?'

Ishukkumuttu listened. The boy must have been delayed today because of the heavy work. Yet why was he so late? Did he not know his father was lying there with no water to drink?

Business in the hotel was extremely brisk. The manager had no time to rest or relax. As he would have immediately seen if he had lifted his head and looked, Chudalamuttu had been standing in the doorway for an hour. No one had seen him. Even if they saw him, they made no sign of recognition. It is only in the morning that people recognise or remember a scavenger. If people are to recognise a scavenger, there is a special door for him to come in by. That door, which is at the back of the premises, was closed. He had called out from behind it. No one had answered. There is a time when people will be listening for the scavenger's call from outside. Then it is enough if he calls out just once or gives a bit of a cough, for the door to be opened.

Chudala jumped over the wall and into the compound, and went and stood at the back of the hotel.

After he had been standing there for a long time, one of the hotel employees came out of the hotel. Failing to recognise him, he asked, 'Who are you? What are you standing here for?' It was the same man who had offered him a *dosha* in the morning.

Chudala said, 'I've come for a little rice-water.'

'It's impossible at this hour. Don't hang around here.'

He cleaned out a large pot and went off again with it. A little later another man came. He too asked him who he was, what he had come for.

'Ishukkumuttu's son.'

'Ishukkumuttu? Who's he?'

'The scavenger for this part of town.'

'Why have you come here now?'

'My father's had nothing to eat all day.'

'Well, there's nothing for you here at the moment. Go and stand by that waste-bin. When they bring the used leaves, help yourself. You'll get plenty.'

The waste-bin he pointed to was full to the brim with leaves. Some left-over food could be recovered from them. Dogs were fighting over it inside the bin.

Chudalamuttu moved away. Deciding to go somewhere else, he opened the door and went out.

The judge lived next door. His father often used to talk of that house, and he thought he would try there.

At the gate stood a gatekeeper. He asked, 'Who are you?'

'I'm Ishukkumuttu's son.'

'Ishukkumuttu? Who's he?'

'The scavenger.'

'What do you want at this hour?'

'I'd like a little rice gruel.'

Chudalamuttu said that his father had been a scavenger in this town for thirty years. The judge had a high regard for him. His father was lying without a drop of water to drink. Could the judge be told of this? The gatekeeper said, 'They are all at their prayers. Nothing can be managed at the moment.'

The noise of a group of people chanting could be heard from inside. Chudalamuttu asked, 'When will their devotions be over?'

'In about three-quarters of an hour.'

His father, his throat dry with thirst, would be calling out for him. Was there at least some fresh water there? Yes, there was water that had been drawn two days earlier. But even if he wanted to take that for drinking he would still have to wait.

Chudalamuttu went to the next house. There, in front of an oil lamp, an old woman in an attitude of prayer was repeating the name of a deity. When Chudala called out 'Would you give me a little water?' the old woman became angry. This was the fourth man to come begging at this inauspicious time!

Chudalamuttu went up and down many flights of steps. By about ten o'clock, when he had been to a number of poorer people's houses, his pot was half-full. He decided to return home now. He had enough rice and water for the old man.

From his experiences of this one day, Chudalamuttu had learnt a lesson or two. When the latrines are unpleasantly full a scavenger will get something. In the evening the latrines are empty. So nobody recognises him.

Chudalamuttu had grown up eating *kanji* and rice that had been brought on top of the scavenger's cart. True enough. But does this mean that he must eat such food every day? If he does his work properly and gets his wages, can he not eat decently? Anyway Chudalamuttu doubted whether he could go on permanently with this same routine. A scavenger who cleaned up dirt was compelled to eat dirt. The next month would be without pay. Two months must pass in the same way. If he went round with this pot in the evening there would be no problem as regards the old man. But what of himself?

Three or four people, respectably dressed, were walking along engaged in animated conversation. Chudala, immersed in thought, passed through the middle of the group. One of them glared at him fiercely and said, 'You stinking creature! Could you not pass by on one side?'

Chudala said nothing. There was a sharp reply on his tongue. But he kept it back. So he ought to go on one side! It seems that he stinks! That which causes him to smell so foul, those fine gentlemen are carrying inside them!

From a big house came the smell of mustard seed being fried for a tasty curry. On both sides houses rose up like symbols of brightness and joy. Yet all this well-being and happiness, thought Chudala, is it not because the latrines are clean? If there were no scavengers, if no man was prepared to become a scavenger, what would become of this town? It would be finished. All these big people would run off holding their noses. They too would be finished. But they know how to find a scavenger. There will never be any lack of scavengers.

It is a fine moonlit night. The wall that can be seen in the distance is the night-soil depot. Beyond that can be seen the black dots that are the scavengers' huts. They lie there lifeless and dilapidated. In one of them, at the northern end, lies Chudalamuttu's father, perhaps calling out for his son.

Chudalamuttu walked on quickly. Eagerly the old man would take and drink this water. Thus he would be satisfied. He would give a long belch. Ah! What a relief! He has a lot to say to his father about people's friendliness and sympathy.

An easy way to get there is by climbing over the wall of the night-soil depot. In the bright moonlight Chudala saw, lying in a pit, the excreta that had been brought that day. He jumped over the pit, leapt over the wall and reached the patch of ground in front of his hut. Inside not a sound was to be heard.

'Father!'

Silence.

'Father!' Not a sound. Chudalamuttu lowered his head and went in. 'Father, are you asleep? I've got some *kanji*.'

Even then there was no reply. Chudala put the pot down and touched his father. His hand felt something as cold as ice. He shuddered. 'Father!' Shaking he called out again. Silence. Chudala shouted at the top of his voice: 'Father!'

Inside the hut a paraffin lamp is burning. In the middle of the room, covered with two or three pieces of cloth, lies the dead body of the old man. Gathered round it, all the scavengers are praying. One man is sitting a little apart from the rest. He is a scavenger who has been converted to Christianity. Chudalamuttu is lying curled up on the floor in another corner of the room.

One man interrupted the praying to ask, 'How old was Ishukkumuttu?' No one could say. Palani, the oldest among them, said, 'As far back as I can remember, he seemed this sort of age.'

After the chanting had gone on for some time Palani took up the point again: 'No one among us ever reached the age he did. If nothing else happens we get typhoid, or cholera, or dysentery, or smallpox. Then it's all over. If it doesn't happen through one of these, then it'll be consumption. Forty is the greatest age we can expect to reach.'

The next topic of discussion was Chudalamuttu's mother. She had been a sweeper in Alleppey. When she died Chudalamuttu was one year old.

The chanting came to an end and they began to talk to each other. Palani said he thought Ishukkumuttu had been a lucky man. No one seemed to understand what he meant by this. Palani explained that his good fortune lay in not being bed-ridden for a long time. Everyone agreed that this was so. Palani went on, 'What do we mean by good fortune? It is to die while walking through the streets.'

Joseph, who was the one sitting apart from the others, could not accept that. He said, 'What sort of good fortune is that?'

Vadivelu saw what Joseph was getting at. From the day of his own conversion Joseph had been advising Vadivelu to change his religion. Vadivelu asked, 'Very well then, what is good fortune? Does it consist of treading the Christian path?'

Rather disdainfully Joseph said, 'Why were we born? To offer praise to God. If we die we need to be saved. One should die consciously accepting the last sacrament.'

The others laughed out loud. Joseph stuck to his convictions and shouted angrily: 'Heathens!'

The cock flapped its wings and crowed. It was midnight. Pichandi asked, 'Shouldn't we be doing more than just sitting around like this?'

This question brought them back to reality and the question of what was to be done. Should they bury Ishukkumuttu that very night or not? In the morning they all had to go to work. Palani asked Chudalamuttu, 'Hey, boy, where is he to be buried?'

Chudala was weeping. Pichandi tried to console him. They would all die; was there anything to be gained by grieving? They should be happy that he had died without suffering. But the pain in Chudalamuttu's heart did not subside. The old man had suffered whatever might be necessary to bring up Chudala since the latter had been one year old. It was for his son that he had lived. Chudala was thinking that it was because he had had no water to drink for the whole of that day that his father had suddenly passed away. He had killed his father.

Once again Palani asked where Chudala wanted him to be buried. Palani explained, 'If we take him to the burial ground we shall have to give the man there something. Then we must give the bearers something, even if it's only water. It will cost about five rupees in all. That's why I asked.'

Shuppu said, 'We must collect that amount. How can we do otherwise?'

Then Joseph, too, spoke up, 'What if we do it at the church? All we shall need there is enough for the burial fee. The present priest is a good man. I'll speak to him. Even if there is no money he'll perform the rites.'

Nobody cared for that idea. Chudala worked out what it would all come to. They needed six rupees. This he did not have. Shuppu said, 'That doesn't matter. You must go in the morning. There will be six rupees somehow.'

Shuppu reminded them of the two or three burials that had taken place among them recently. How were those expenses met? They must go and ask at the houses where they worked. If they asked they would get the money. The dead body would have to lie there a day or two. That way at least there would be a chance of their having the satisfaction that it had been done properly.

Chudalamuttu thought back over his experiences of that day; the reasons why the old man had suddenly died. He thought of relating them. But he did not have the strength. He simply said, 'I cannot ask.'

Again they all put their heads together but failed to reach any conclusion. Once more the cock-crow reminded them that time was getting short. Palani insisted that they must come to a decision. What did Chudala have to say about it?

'Let's bury him somewhere in the compound before dawn,' said Pichandi.

'Shan't we be breaking the law?' asked Shuppu.

'Oh! Who will know? It'll be alright if we keep it to ourselves.'

Vadivelu asked Pichandi, 'Didn't we bury Palani's wife there some time back? We could bury Ishukkumuttu under the big cashew-nut tree.'

It seemed a good idea. Palani agreed and said, 'Let's do that, then.'

For a while they sat there without saying anything to each other. Palani got up and went out to stretch himself. Joseph gave a long yawn. Andi rubbed his eyes. All of them were having difficulty in keeping awake. Palani broke the silence with 'I say! Will there be any trouble?'

Pichandi agreed to accept the responsibility. 'But no one must breathe a word about it outside our group.'

Pichandi made Chudalamuttu stand up. He took a look at his father's face. He lay there as if asleep. Until this day there had been somebody who wished Chudalamuttu to live. There had been somebody for Chudalamuttu to be afraid of. From now on he need not say the word 'Father'. There was no one to call him 'Son'.

All together they picked up the body and took it outside to bathe it. When they were bringing it back, the old man seemed to be smiling. It was more than Chudalamuttu could bear.

There was no cloth to cover the dead body. Pichandi and Shuppu brought one. Meanwhile Vallinayakam and Shivanandi picked up their spades and went to the depot. Then all the dogs in the depot began to bark at once.

With a view to giving him the six feet of earth he was entitled to, they took Ishukkumuttu up there and decided on a suitable spot. After the body had been put into the grave Chudalamuttu scooped up a few handfuls of earth. With breaking heart he managed to utter the word 'Father'.

When the grave had been filled in and everybody had gone away some dogs came up to find out what had been going on there.

The residents were complaining to the manager of the hotel at the road junction. The scavenger had come and gone but it was impossible to enter the latrine, which was in a filthy state. One of the hotel workers mentioned that the scavenger had been there the previous evening.

There was also trouble at the judge's house. Although the scavenger had been there too the latrine was not clean. Thus in several houses people were feeling put out. And once again the scavenger became a topic of conversation.

At midday Chudalamuttu was on his way to the night-soil depot, pushing his refuse cart. He noticed that several people held their noses and gave him a wide berth. It was a foul-smelling object. The muscles round his father's mouth had always been pulled in as if to close the nostrils. To the same end, his top lip had been curled upwards. How had that come about? Maybe it took that shape on the occasion when he first went into a latrine with his shovel and bucket. The old man's father had not been a scavenger. But one generation of scavengers created another. Without his being aware of it, his face would now take on a bad shape.

The night-soil depot was very busy at that time. Numerous carts were coming in. Chudalamuttu, too, came in through the gate, weak and exhausted. The previous day he had neither eaten nor slept. In addition, on the previous day an important event had taken place. Noticing how worn-out he looked, Pichandi came up, took his cart and pushed it up to the pit. As he lifted the lid and turned it to face the pit, he asked, 'Hey, boy! Why so little? Didn't you do a full round today?'

'I did.'

Pichandi thought of a joke – a scavenger's joke! 'Yesterday everybody must have had very little to eat.'

When Shuppu, who was standing nearby, heard it, he laughed. He wasn't complaining; today he hadn't had enough to fill one cart. Then Joseph said that in Europeans' houses the job was easy. In that way the more experienced scavengers explained how the latrines of various communities differed. After being on the job for two days Chudalamuttu also had something to contribute. Though he could hardly bear his fatigue, he said, 'In all the latrines it lay in heaps. I took some from each. You ought to see them all. Big and fat – they all eat like white ants.' Pichandi was cleaning out Chudalamuttu's cart. Chudala went on: 'They forget that it is human beings who must fetch all this. When they go into the latrine they make it filthy everywhere and so the scavenger has a hard time of it.'

'And if it is human beings who have to collect it, must they not eat?' asked Vadivelu.

Shivanandi took up the point, 'Eat! After over-eating and fouling up the latrine they all find fault with the scavenger. That's what gets me.'

After thinking about it carefully Palani gave his opinion: 'They simply want to eat. They don't think about the latrine. That's the trouble.'

Another scavenger, with ten years' experience, said, 'In my ward 75 per cent don't seem to digest anything.'

On that, too, Palani, the eldest among them, had something to say: 'The well-to-do eat without any consideration for their stomachs. They don't do a stroke of work. So they digest nothing. The poor man eats anything. So his digestion, too, is poor.'

Chudalamuttu, who had been taking all of this in, said, 'Why is it that they forget that we too are human beings?'

'We fail to realise ourselves that we are creatures of flesh and blood,' said Pichandi.

Another scavenger added, 'Our womenfolk realise it.' They all burst out laughing.

'The women in these big houses have no sense of shame,' said Pichandi.

'Do they show this only in their dealings with us?'

Chudalamuttu did not know what this meant. He still had to learn about such things.

They had all finished their work. For all of them there would be something to eat when they went home. Some of them would have eaten already. What about Chudalamuttu?

Pichandi asked, 'Chudala, is there anything for you at home?' He did not reply. 'In that case let's go home.' Chudalamuttu and Pichandi went together to Pichandi's house.

The following day, from the various houses he called at, Chudalamuttu got a little money – two annas or so. He neither asked for it nor expected it. On that day all the householders were waiting for him.

Chudalamuttu had a lot of work to do on this occasion. Nevertheless he returned with satisfaction. He doubted whether anyone cared about a scavenger who did his work well; they simply wouldn't realise he was doing his job. When the stench from the latrines reached the top floor they would enquire about it. If he made them remember the existence of the latrine – the scavenger would not be forgotten.

Thus the scavenger was not without power and influence. But he did not appreciate his power. The judge thought well of Chudalamuttu. When his father died he showed much sympathy. He gave him four annas. Though finding fault at first, the wealthy Reddiar was careful not to quarrel with him. Fine. The scavenger was not all that insignificant a person. People fear him. If the latrines are not in a very clean state – big people have occasion to speak a little less haughtily to the scavenger.

Chudalamuttu learnt fast. But there were still many things to learn. There was also a lot to do.

At the night-soil depot there was no one to be seen, no sign of life. Was it time for them all to go? He wasn't as late as all that. There was some special reason. As he came up to the gate an unbearable smell of putrefaction reached his nose.

Beneath the cashew-nut tree lay something red and decaying. The ground had been disturbed. Beyond it some dogs stood growling. The other scavengers stood at a distance, looking. Chudalamuttu jumped over the trenches to get there.

The dogs have scratched at the ground where Ishukkumuttu's dead body is buried and have uncovered half of it. They have bitten, torn and mauled the face and neck. The eyes seem to be staring. They are looking at him. From them drips a bluish liquid.

Pichandi came up and took hold of him.

If a corpse is buried and covered over, some sorrow too will be buried. But even that consolation is denied the scavenger. Even after the body has decayed the son must see it yet again.

The other scavengers have another problem, however. Whether it is dogs or worms that get Ishukkumuttu's body, it is all one to them. They have buried a dead body in the night-soil depot. How are they going to explain that?

Shuppu spoke: 'I said at the time that we should take it to the burial ground.'

'I told you then that the hole was not deep enough,' said Shivanandi.

Joseph reminded them that he had said they should take it to the church for burial. If they had done so, would this calamity have occurred? Chudalamuttu must find a way out. Because of his father they had all been exposed to this danger.

Suddenly, as when a stone is thrown among a flock of crows, the whole crowd ran off in all directions. Some jumped over the wall. Others hid among the bushes. Only Pichandi and Chudalamuttu stood their ground. The overseer, who was cycling along the road, came up. Chudalamuttu walked to the road and Pichandi followed.

The overseer looked Chudalamuttu sternly up and down and asked him in a severe tone of voice: 'What is it lying there?'

Chudalamuttu said meekly, 'Father's dead body.'

'How did it come to be there?'

Feeling guilty, Chudalamuttu said nothing. It was something that ought not to have been done; it had been done. What answer could he give?

'It was buried very deep,' said Pichandi.

The overseer flared up with anger. 'Who else had a hand in burying it?'

Why should all of them be made to carry the guilt for what was his own fault? Yet how could he avoid telling the truth? Chudalamuttu was in a dilemma.

The overseer abused all of them very severely. He'd seen them all jumping and running out of the way. He'd teach the whole lot of them a good lesson. Let them remember! Then he got on his bicycle and rode off.

While Pichardi was digging a hole Chudalamuttu was busy dragging out the corpse, which was still half buried in the ground. Caught with a blow from the spade, the distended belly burst open. One hand came off.

After working without a break for quite some time they got Ishukkumuttu buried again. Now they faced a new problem. There was the matter of their scavenger friends and the trouble they were in. Pichandi was the only one who could help Chudalamuttu. Pichandi consoled him, saying he would always be a friend to him. Leaning his head on Pichandi's shoulder, Chudalamuttu sobbed. Pichandi, too, wept. Then he wiped away his tears. 'Don't cry, lad. Is there not always a solution?'

'You must be as an elder brother to me. You are the only help I have.'

'Even if I lose my job I'll stand by you.'

All the scavengers talked the matter over and decided to send Palani, Pichandi and Chudalamuttu to the overseer to speak for them.

The toddy shop!

It is a thatched building standing by the side of the road and surrounded by a fence made of coconut leaves and bamboo. It is divided into a number of rooms, each of them a separate unit.

Business has quietened down a little. It is after ten at night but it is not time for the regulars to leave. In all the rooms animated conversation can be heard.

On the verandah of the room at the western end Shuppu, Joseph, Sundiran and Vadivelu are sitting in a circle away from the door. In the middle are four empty bottles, two full ones and some cups. There are similar groups of scavengers outside the other rooms too.

It is the scavengers' payday. No matter how much noise there is, the proprietors do not complain. This is the day when the scavengers enjoy themselves.

Shuppu asked Vadivelu, 'Hey, how much pay did you get?'

'Eight. How about you?'

'I got seven and a half.'

'Seven and a half? Why's that?'

'Can't say.'

Joseph had received nine rupees. The previous month it was only six and a half. Then Sundiran mentioned something that was puzzling him: 'What should our wages be really?'

Taking the toddy bottle and refilling the cups, Shuppu said, 'Only the overseer knows that.'

'But this month we've all had our wages cut. It's for burying old Ishukkumuttu,' said Joseph.

Sundiran agreed, 'Yes. That's it.'

On the verandah of the next room were Palani and his friends. Shuppu called out to him, 'I say, Palani! Did you have a special drop in wages this month?'

'Yes, I did,' replied Palani.

Palani and his friends got up and went to join Shuppu's group. The topic was one that interested all of them. Those sitting in front of the other shops also got up and joined them. Altogether there were now ten or twelve scavengers in the group. As a result of their burying Ishukkumuttu they had all had a cut in their pay.

'Why should we all lose money like this for nothing?' asked Joseph.

'What else can we do?' said Palani.

'Chudala must make up what we've lost.'

Palani laughed. Where was Chudalamuttu to get it from? It was only a few days since he had started work. He would get no pay for the first two months. Shuppu got angry. 'I said at the time that we should take him to the burial ground. I want my money.'

'Who is to give it?' asked Palani.

'Anyone you like.'

Pichandi was standing a little apart from the rest smoking a *beedi*. He said, 'Then you get it!'

'I'll get it,' said Shuppu. 'As sure as I'm a man, I'll get it.'

'Not even your father could get it.'

'What's that! Are you talking about my father?'

'And if I am, what'll you do about it?'

Shuppu leapt at Pichandi. Palani grabbed hold of Pichandi and Avuda held Shuppu. The two of them began to curse and swear at each other. No one knew who was abusing whom. The proprietors came out.

At this juncture, nobody knew from where, four policemen turned up. Everything went quiet. They gave a blow each to Pichandi, Palani and Shuppu. All were standing shaking, with their hands held together.

So they lost what was left of their pay. Nor was that all. A part of their next month's wages, too, was spoken for. Together they all left the shop. For a long time they walked as if they had no tongues in their mouths.

It was Sundiran who broke the silence by asking, 'Wasn't it Vadivelu who got beaten last month?'

One of them confirmed that this was so. 'These policemen wait for our payday. It's the same every month. Where did that lot come from?'

They all agreed that this was true. It had been Palani's experience ever since he had become a scavenger.

Joseph said, 'They remember the day and lie in wait for us.'

But what remedy was there? Absolutely none. What if the latrines belonging to the policemen's houses were not emptied? More beatings! Pichandi had something to say. In fact he gave a speech. All the scavengers must unite. Then they would find out how much each scavenger should have each month; they would get that amount in full. There would be no need to fear any policeman.

Pichandi used to make this speech every month on payday, and on this occasion, too, he made it. They all listened. They decided that all the scavengers and sweepers should combine to form a union. But Pichandi had one more thing to say. That, too, he used to say each time: 'I have just told you that we must stand united and so on. Tomorrow the overseer will know. This means I shall get two blows from his cane and half a rupee knocked off my pay. For that's what I get every month for saying what I've just told you.'

The Union

Going by the backs of the houses and along the narrow lanes of Chandanakkow Ward a scavenger is to be seen dressed in vest and shorts, wearing a diagonally folded kerchief on his head and carrying a bucket and shovel. He has a slim moustache. He is quite sturdy and well-built. His vest and shorts are neat and clean. One can see at a glance that he is no ordinary scavenger. If it were not for the tools he is carrying, one would doubt whether he really was a scavenger.

His thoughts are on a matter of some importance. He has plenty to think about. He is a person who sees and understands things. He is not coming to work after getting drunk and incapable the previous evening and laying down to sleep somewhere or other by the side of the road. Yesterday he had a bath; he ate; he slept. Today, too, he will take a bath, eat well, sleep. If we look at him closely once again, we shall observe that in the depths of his eyes the cringing and deferential expression of a scavenger is not to be seen. He is a determined sort of person. He will not bow his head unnecessarily.

You will not care for a scavenger like that. You definitely will not like a scavenger who takes a bath every day, a scavenger who shaves, a scavenger who wears a *dhoti* or shorts that he has either washed or had laundered. 'What a lady-killer!' your womenfolk will say. If she sees him a young woman will not be able to enter or leave a latrine. The scavenger you like to see must be a drunkard; there must be no system or order in his life. He must always be in some sort of trouble.

This scavenger, however, is Chudalamuttu. He does his work properly. No one takes liberties with him. But he shows respect for the people of every household. He has learnt many things from those who are higher in the social scale. So, in this short time, he has come a long way. There are still many things in life for him to achieve.

But in that ward there was nobody who was not in some way disturbed or put out by him. Once he caused the honourable judge a bit of trouble. In that gentleman's latrine, which has no roof, there is a hole in the side facing the lane. The latrine can be cleaned from the lane itself. The door to that hole had come off. Even though Chudalamuttu asked for a new door to be fixed the judge did nothing about it. One night it rained heavily. The next day there was no work for Chudalamuttu to do in the latrine. It was not his job to clean the lane. Someone filed a complaint. The judge has still not forgotten the shame he felt on account of this lawsuit.

See what a danger there is in a scavenger having intelligence and a sense of hygiene! If you live in a place where there is such a scavenger, is it not an affront to your dignity?

No one cares very much for Chudalamuttu. Yet on a particular day they are all waiting to give him money. He has no need to ask. Everyone is well aware of that day; no one forgets it.

Chudalamuttu has learnt both to make money and to save it. He has money put by. This is an important lesson he has learnt from other people. He is thinking of increasing his savings. Another important lesson.

However even now the overseer makes life difficult for him, as for all the others. Even after all this, he still does not know what his real wages are. What is certain is that he is not getting the full amount of pay due to him.

A number of scavengers met together to consider this problem. Pichandi proposed his customary solution.

'We must all band together,' he said.

For some days, while doing his rounds, Chudalamuttu had also been thinking about this. It seemed to him that if they were united they could achieve many things. They would be paid their wages in full. They would get their pay without giving part of it to the overseer. They could have shorter hours of work. Because he personally had great influence with the scavengers, he could see certain other advantages. Chudalamuttu planned to live a long time!

'The *coir* workers have an association,' said Chudalamuttu. 'Carpenters and so on have an association. We, too, need one. Only then can we accomplish anything.'

They were all of the same mind. The scavengers, too, needed an association. They entrusted Chudalamuttu with the responsibility of forming an association of that sort. Chudalamuttu agreed to take it on.

In Chandanakkow there is a man who knows how to set up such an association. His house is one where Chudalamuttu works. One day they must get hold of him and form an association. With this decision the meeting is adjourned for that particular day.

From that day on Chudalamuttu is constantly thinking about this matter. If an association is formed there will certainly be an important role for Chudalamuttu to fill in it. All his fellow workers will be under him. If they are under him . . . then stemming from that there is something else. In addition to the overseer, will not the municipality also be somewhat in awe of him? Chudalamuttu had an idea: what if he met the initial expenses from his own pocket?

After the meeting and the speeches were over, it seemed that ideas that had lain half-formed in their minds took on a clearer shape. In reality the speaker only said what they had often thought. But when they heard it they realised there were important things even in their lives: they had responsibilities; above all they were not without power.

Each scavenger feels a sense of pride which he has not experienced before. Now each scavenger can speak like that. The whole town depends on him. He can make all the people of the town fear him.

On that day there arose a feeling of class-consciousness. It was the day on which the scavengers of Alleppey town proclaimed something in a single voice. The sound of it echoed on all sides. The hearts of the town fathers will quake. A huge concentration of power has started to move. Now it is calling aloud. Tomorrow . . . it will begin to act.

So on that day the scavengers' union was founded. One by one they signed the form – Pichandi, Palani, Shivanandi, Vadivelu –

all of them. All, that is, except Chudalamuttu. Though it was he who called the meeting, Chudalamuttu was simply sitting in a corner. No one had noticed. Will the eagerness to set up an association wait for one man? They all joined. They all became members of the union. Chudalamuttu's mind was troubled. The crush and noise around the chairman's seat seemed to him a sort of madness.

Chudalamuttu could not make sense of what the speaker had said. It seemed to Chudalamuttu that he had said that if there were a union a man who belonged to it could not act as an individual. In that case, thought Chudalamuttu, there would be no advantage in this association. Nothing would be achieved. A few of the speaker's statements are reverberating in Chudalamuttu's ears. It seems that the scavenger is an important person! He can't make any sense of that. Must he not try to get out of this in some way? If the scavenger has some importance . . . must he remain a scavenger for ever? This association was for those who would always remain scavengers. It was fine for someone who was content to lie in dirt. That was not Chudalamuttu's intention . . . Another of the speaker's remarks had been to the effect that they must take their rights by force! That means getting involved in disputes with their superiors, does it not? All this talk by the speaker about their superiors . . . but maybe they will be without a job tomorrow. He also said something about God and fate. No, this association was dangerous. Nevertheless, all were joining.

Such was the confusion in Chudalamuttu's mind. The high pitch of excitement and the scavengers' enthusiasm seemed ridiculous to him. Had they nothing in their heads? It was quite a show. Everything would be drained into this enthusiasm and come to nothing.

Once again the whole place began to reverberate with slogans. Unsuspected energy became apparent in that noisy assembly. These were not emaciated faces of men suffering from privation and hard work. What a difference! Their eyes shone! Their faces lit up. When they shouted the slogans, their raised hands, with palms turned upwards towards the sky, seemed to be made of iron. They had become one. Now – now – they would strike and crush many things.

Chudalamuttu, too, felt like jumping up to join them in

shouting aloud. But he was afraid: that force was crushing him too. It was destroying his plans. Unnoticed by anyone, Chudala-muttu went out.

When all of them had become members the meeting resumed. The next thing was to elect the executive committee of the union. That day's chairman was the chairman. When they began to nominate the other members someone mentioned Chudalamut-tu's name. He had not joined. He was not even present.

The chairman was flabbergasted. The organiser of the meeting had stolen away! The rest of those present were equally aston-ished.

That night was another important night in Chudalamuttu's life. Some of the things he had heard in the speeches earlier that day, some of the slogans that had been shouted, were echoing in his ears.

However he was determined that none of the generation that followed him should ever be a scavenger. He was positive that he would never make scavengers of his children. In that case was there any need for him to join this union?

Let them fight. Will he not get the benefits their efforts bring? With such thoughts Chudalamuttu consoles himself. When he sees his friends tomorrow he knows how to satisfy them. They are poor fellows. They cannot keep away from him. When they need a bit of cash, is there anyone else who can give it?

The next day, when he was on his way to work, the first person he met was the overseer, Keshava Pillai. The latter gave him a rather contemptuous look. 'What's this about your union?'

Chudalamuttu's heart pounded: 'I didn't . . . It's . . .' He was unable to give a reply that made any sense.

'Mm. The president is making enquiries. It was a mistake to employ you. You're a scoundrel. I should have known all along. It's my own stupidity.'

'It – I'm not in it. I . . .' Only by giving a lengthy explanation could Chudalamuttu demonstrate his innocence. Nothing coher-ent or systematic came out. He had never realised he would be faced with a crisis of this sort. As a result he had not worked out

what reply he should give. In any case the overseer did not have the patience to listen; he was too angry.

Chudalamuttu had a feeling he would lose his job — a real calamity. This could all have been avoided. What folly it was that had led to it! But he had never imagined it would be like this if a union were to be formed. When he saw the president of the municipality how would he explain it all?

Such were Chudalamuttu's thoughts as he went round doing his work that day. He made a firm decision as to how he should present his explanation and on everything he should say. He learnt his speech by heart and rehearsed it several times.

In the evening Chudalamuttu went and saw the overseer in his house. He begged that he should not suffer for what had happened. The overseer's anger was not assuaged. He would show him what was what. A decision had been made. The president was in agreement and it was all decided.

Chudalamuttu did not know what to do. A paper packet containing money was placed at the overseer's feet. But the latter would not agree to help him. It was not a matter to be agreed on. The president was exceedingly angry. With great reluctance the overseer finally agreed to speak to the president on his behalf.

The president was sitting at home in his office. Chudalamuttu went through the gate and stood in a corner of the front yard, while the overseer went inside. Through the window Chudalamuttu was able to see the president and the overseer talking. What an anxious few minutes it was! A fire burned in his stomach. His whole body was hot. He sat down, stood up, walked about; he watched their gestures. Was there any room for hope? His whole future was being decided there.

Finally the president came out. Chudalamuttu could hear his heart beat. Every moment was unbearable. Was he coming to tell him that he was being dismissed?

The face of Keshava Pillai, who was following, gave nothing away. The president's face was flushed with annoyance. He asked Keshava Pillai: 'Is this him, Keshava Pillai?'

'Yes!' said Keshava Pillai.

'Mm. Yes. He looks a rather insolent fellow, don't you think?'

Scratching his head, Keshava Pillai mumbled, 'Yes, but — he's very poor.'

The president looked Chudalamuttu up and down. 'Are you the one who organised the meeting?'

Chudalamuttu could not utter a sound. He forgot all that he had learned off by heart for the occasion. He felt he was going to pass out.

'Do we need such scoundrels, Keshava Pillai? Several people in Chandanakkow have told me that he gets a bit above himself. The judge and the Reddiar are among those who say so. Well, what about your association?'

'I didn't join, sir.' Involuntarily that sentence jumped out from Chudalamuttu's lips. Phew! What a relief.

'Didn't join? How's that? Wasn't his name on the printed notices as the organiser?'

'Yes,' said Keshava Pillai. 'But while the meeting was in progress he left. I asked the other scavengers about it.'

The president asked Chudalamuttu: 'Is that correct?'

Chudalamuttu was relieved to be able to reply, 'Yes.'

Now Chudalamuttu was not longer tongue-tied. The president went on to ask, 'Why was it that you left?'

'What the speaker said after the meeting began didn't seem right.'

'What was it he said?'

Chudalamuttu thought for a while and then said, 'He spoke ill of the authorities. He said we must enter into a dispute with them to get our wages. But you see, sir, my tongue can't bring itself to say that the people we work for are all thieves – and fat, over-fed ones at that. He said that God was a thief, too. Then I dashed out. I didn't want to hear anymore of that sort of thing.'

The president turned to Keshava Pillai: 'You see. They are leading these poor fellows astray!'

Chudalamuttu got a bit bolder and went on: 'When the speaker said they must fight those above them, that they must strike and crush something, he asked them to say in a single voice, "We will crush them all." He got them all to say it. They all shouted with fists clenched, as if to strike. I took no part in this.'

'All those things are said in your notice. Why did you put your name to it?' asked the president.

Assuming an air of innocence, Chudalamuttu said, 'The president of the artisans union told me to sign. I signed.'

After a short pause the municipal president said, 'Who are those who went?'

It was Keshava Pillai who answered that one, 'They all went.'

'Who are the ringleaders?'

Chudalamuttu gave the names of Vadivelu, Shivanandi and a few others like them.

Keshava Pillai had a few more things to say. 'If he wishes, Chudalamuttu can break up this association.'

'How can you break it up?' the president asked Chudalamuttu.

'They all owe Chudalamuttu money,' Keshava Pillai. 'When they are short he lends them a few annas. Because of this, they will all withdraw if he asks them. It was because his name was on the notice that they went to the meeting.'

'Does he have some money put by, then?'

Bashfully Chudalamuttu said that he did have a few coppers.

Keshava Pillai continued: 'He knows how to save and look after money. He doesn't drink toddy. He's after having a plot of land and a small house.'

'Ha! So that's it, eh?'

'Yes.'

'Fine! That's good. That's how to improve yourself. But don't get led astray like this. Right then; if you behave yourself, I can also help you.'

Keshava Pillai made a suggestion: 'Let him bring here all the money he's got put by. He can also hand over all that he gets from now on. When it has mounted up sufficiently we must buy a plot of land and a hut for him.'

'That can be done. If necessary, I'll give something from my own pocket. Anyone with a wish to improve himself should be helped. I'm glad to see this.'

Keshava Pillai had a few words with Chudalamuttu. 'Tomorrow you must bring all the money you've got put by; you understand?' Chudala agreed. It seemed to him a good way of doing things. The president added a warning: 'But he must break up this association. How about it?'

Chudalamuttu replied, 'I shall try!'

'That's not enough. You must break it up. Keshava Pillai will help.'

So Chudalamuttu went off happy, not only because his anxiety

was ended, but also because a good way had been found for him to
go up in the world.

Keshava Pillai and Chudalamuttu put their heads together and
worked out a plan. Chudalamuttu undertook to carry out to the
letter his part in it. On his side the overseer undertook to see that
Chudalamuttu would benefit from the plan. From now on they
must be on friendly terms with each other.

But the next day Chudalamuttu arrived at and left the night-soil
depot earlier than anyone. In that way he was able to avoid seeing
his friends there. That day he did not go home. It was the same the
next day. That evening the overseer asked him: 'Who did you see?
How did it all turn out?'

How was Chudalamuttu to reply? He had not spoken to
anybody. If he were to see them, would he have a proper answer to
give? How would he look them in the face and speak to them? Not
only that; he had no idea as to what answer he should give. For the
last two days he had been turning it over in his mind. He would
certainly have to reply to their questions – for they would
assuredly ask a few questions. Chudalamuttu was faced with a
difficult moral problem.

But for how many days could he hide like this? Could he go on
not seeing them or speaking to them? Chudalamuttu said to the
overseer, 'That business – I am working out a plan.'

Keshava Pillai got angry. 'When is it to be put into practice?
Are you waiting till the association is running smoothly and is well
established?'

'No, not that. Are they people with the ability to think? They are
very annoyed with me. After a couple of days their anger will cool
down. Then it will be easier.'

That reply seemed to make sense to Keshava Pillai.

Anyway, after two days had passed, Chudalamuttu did see
three or four of the other scavengers. It was when he was in the
night-soil depot. When he got there, Shivanandi, Pichandi and
Vadivelu were there too. Chudalamuttu saw them when he was
some way off. His heartbeat quickened. How was he to face them?
Still, he plucked up courage and went in. Chudalamuttu's face was
a sight to be seen. In spite of all his efforts it turned pale. In it were

reflected all the things that were going on in his mind. Chudalamuttu did his work as if there was no one there. After the others
had said one or two things quietly among themselves, Pichandi
went up to Chudalamuttu and asked, 'Where have you been? We
couldn't find you anywhere.'

Chudalamuttu's tongue felt dry as he stammered, 'I – I – but I
was here.'

By then Shivanandi and Vadivelu had also come up. Shivanandi's voice registered astonishment as he asked, 'What! Who's this?
Chudalamuttu? You're a fine one. Having got us all to the
meeting, you slunk off.'

'Slunk off? Where to?' said Vadivelu. 'Oh! He didn't join
because he had no money for the fee.'

Pichandi asked him: 'Didn't you come to work yesterday and
the day before?'

'Yes, I came,' answered Chudala. 'I wasn't feeling so good.'

'Why didn't you join the union? You went off before the meeting
was over.'

Chudalamuttu got hold of himself sufficiently to speak. He
could now hold his head up. He said, 'Brother Pichandi, I'll give it
to you straight. I didn't like it at all. What exactly did that speech
amount to? Just a lot of shouting and abuse. Is this what is meant
by a union?'

'What was wrong with the speech?' asked Shivanandi.

'It was the speech of a blackguard. Isn't he simply trying to ruin
the livelihood of poor people like us? If we do as he says we shall
finish up in jail, I tell you, in jail.'

'Then are we not to speak of our problems?' asked Vadivelu.

'Is this the way to go about it? Did he not say that we should
attack our superiors? You'll see! Not one of those who joined the
union will have work. The municipal president knows about it.'

Pichandi asked disingenuously, 'But wasn't it you who asked
the speaker along? Why was that?'

'Did I know he was a man of this sort?'

Shivanandi lost his temper. 'What's wrong with him? He's a
man. Your president's tricks and the overseer's won't work with
him. He's been to jail many times for the sake of the skilled
workers!'

Chudalamuttu, too, gave the impression of being rather angry. 'What was it he said? That we must improve ourselves?'

'And what else?'

'If you are a man you must have a certain amount of common sense. You must be able to understand what you hear. Did he say we must become better by giving up our jobs as scavengers? Should he not teach us that we should save the money we earn and not squander it, that we should have faith in God, that we should not drink, that we should respect our superiors? I thought he would say all these things.'

'But isn't all that he said the truth?' said Shivanandi.

'Then take warning. One by one the president of the municipality will destroy you. Just mark my words.'

Neither Pichandi, nor Shivanandi, nor Vadivelu had anything else to say. They wanted to refute what Chudalamuttu had said, but they did not know how to do so. They had a high opinion of Chudalamuttu's intelligence and of his understanding of these matters. Nevertheless they felt that what he had said about their union president was not right. They had not realised that they would lose their jobs. Would they be out of work because they had joined a union?

'Did you see the president?' asked Shivanandi.

'I did,' said Chudalamuttu. 'What he said was that he would finish the whole lot of you. He would have done it the day after the meeting. The overseer and I said, "They are poor people. They'll resign from the union. You must excuse them." And so on. After hearing what we said he calmed down a bit.' Chudalamuttu finished cleaning his refuse cart and then went off straight away.

Pichandi, Shivanandi and Vadivelu gave the matter some careful thought. Pichandi said that in his opinion there might be something in what Chudalamuttu said, adding, 'For saying that we needed a union my wages were cut.'

Kelu and Pappu, two scavengers who lived near the seashore, had been suspended because of a complaint that had been made against them. There was talk that Vadivelu and Shivanandi would be laid off. Arrangements were being made for some scavengers to be brought from Tirunelveli in Madras State across the border. If that happened, then all the existing workers would be dismissed.

There was no peace of mind in any of the scavengers' houses. All their wives were asking why they had joined the union. It was the union that was to blame for everything. Payday had come and gone. Nobody had been paid. Formerly they had been able to get a small loan from Chudalamuttu once in a while. Now it was no use going to him. He would not give anything.

'I'm broke. And even if I wasn't, the president told me not to give money to anyone who had joined the union. So my advice to you is to buy a bit of low-grade rice and live on that.'

This is the sort of response they would get from Chudalamuttu. Among the scavengers hunger increased considerably, and with it discontent. One result was that the latrines were not kept clean. There were complaints against many of the men. Several were warned that they would lose their jobs.

A memorandum was submitted on behalf of the union. A pamphlet was published setting out their immediate demands. The union president made two requests in writing to see the municipal chairman. On three occasions he went to his residence. But he still did not manage to see him.

All a union can do is submit demands and then, after discussion, come to an agreement. Was this an affair of more than a few days?

As a result of their discussions at the night-soil depot, in the toddy shop, in front of their homes, the scavengers were positive about one thing. Either they must withdraw from the union, or they must be prepared to endure any amount of hardship. But on one thing they were all agreed: unity was essential.

So things were in a rather confused state. The hardships became more and more difficult to bear. One day they heard that the suspended Pappu had been taken on again. He had been paid his wages the day after he left the union. The next day Joseph backed out. In that way, within four or five days one-third of the scavengers withdrew from the union. All of them got their pay. Shortly afterwards it became known that the union president had been arrested as the suspect in a rape case.

Chudalamuttu and Keshava Pillai won. The room that had been the union office was now a barber's shop. The municipal workers no longer had a union. The president of the municipality presented Chudalamuttu with a *dhoti* and upper cloth and a New Year gift of two rupees. He also gave him a warning: 'In future, don't allow anything of this sort to happen. You understand?'

'Yes!'

But Keshava Pillai, who saw a lot of the scavengers, had something more to say. The desire to have a union had taken root among the scavengers. It would not fade away.

'What shall we do about it?' asked the president.

'There is only one way to deal with it; but it must be left in our hands.'

That seemed fine to the president, and he gave Keshava Pillai permission to do all that was necessary and agreed that any expenditure involved would be borne by the municipality.

Within a month, in a theatre in Alleppey, another union of scavengers and sweepers was formed. It was a *sanyasi* who performed the inaugural ceremony. Presiding over the function was one of the big traders of the town.

That day a sumptuous feast was held at the town hall for the scavengers and sweepers. They each received a *dhoti*. After that the big meeting took place. There they heard many fine speakers, but without understanding a word of what was said. Someone was saying something. None of it had anything to do with them or with matters that concerned them. What if the esteemed *sanyasi* said they should not drink toddy? They already knew it was bad. When he counselled them to pray to God, they saw nothing new in his advice. When he said that their superiors had feelings of sympathy for them – that, too, they heard every day. However, because of their strong desire to have a union, they all became members of this one. The subscriptions were all generously paid by the municipality. Just look at the kindness of their bosses! Keshava Pillai became president. When an executive committee, too, had been elected, the meeting closed with the singing of the national song of Travancore.

That day their dinner included a special kind of dessert. During the meeting the fans above them were turning. There was no chance of anybody feeling any physical discomfort. But when they left after the meeting no one spoke to anyone. What an air of melancholy! Yet not so much melancholy as weakness. Physical weakness? Not really, for it was a weakness of the soul rather than the body. It was as if their life-force had been changed, taken away, stolen. It was as if they had lost something very dear to them.

Maybe in the depths of their hearts a subdued class-conscious-ness was roaring like the sea itself. If one looked carefully at their faces one could see the dissatisfaction that lay deep within them.

See how nowadays, religion, with its consoling message of life after death, makes its approach with so much more enthusiasm and sincerity than in former days; are not even the powers-that-be willing to make concessions? Do not big millionaires donate huge sums to charitable institutions? Thinkers are trying to revise their philosophies! Some people go so far as to say there is communism in the Bible. What lies behind all this? It is because the reverberations of the dissatisfaction lying in the depths of the hearts of millions of people in the world can be heard! It is greater than the roar of the mighty ocean!

With the look of one who had won a complete victory, Keshava Pillai followed respectfully a little behind the municipal president. The two of them were engaged in cheerful conversation. Walking behind Keshava Pillai, Chudalamuttu said not a word. Deep down, for some strange reason, he was not happy.

Is he, too, not downtrodden? Whatever the nature of the burden, is he not bearing it too? Perhaps he, too, has the feeling that he has lost something.

Marriage

The night-soil depot. None of the scavengers had yet arrived, for it was too soon. Only two cats were standing next to the trenches.

In the shade of a mango tree that spread its branches in one corner of the compound a lover stood close to his girlfriend. Her head bent down, she was waiting expectantly; but he did not dare to hold her close! In his heart he was eager to embrace her and kiss her cheek, but he lacked the necessary courage.

'There is something I . . .'

Chudalamuttu was too tongue-tied to be able to say what he felt. Slowly Valli raised her head and looked at him tenderly. It was as if there was fear mingled with his love. She laughed a little. If he wanted, could he not take her in his arms and dance? But he was afraid even to touch her. Was there any need for him to ask permission?

Haltingly Chudalamuttu spoke again: 'I have . . . something . . . to say.'

With a smile she asked, 'What is it?'

Chudalamuttu did not reply. His lips trembled. He had a lot to say. He had thought it all out. But now he had forgotten everything.

Seeing his confusion, Valli could not control herself. She burst out laughing. As she did, he came out with, 'I'm going to have a house built.' That was the wrong way to begin. That was not what he wished to say first.

'Is that what you wanted to tell me? What was so difficult about it?' she asked.

He went all bashful. Still in a state of confusion he said, 'No, I've decided to buy a house and compound.'

'To buy a house and compound? What for?'

'It's for you.' Chudalamuttu looked intently at Valli's face to see what her reaction would be.

'It's you it's for.' These words had come from the depths of his heart. It was on the day he met her that the compound and house had taken shape in his mind. The words touched Valli's heart too. She understood their import. She looked down once again and was going to say something.

With one hand Chudala held her close to him. With the other he lifted her head and, as she was eagerly waiting for him to do, kissed her. All the wild flowers in the compound waved their heads. The crows scratching and picking in the trenches called to each other as if they were talking about this love scene.

He said that the house and compound he was going to buy were for her. That was how she took it. But it was not actually for her. Chudalamuttu had not thought of making a house and compound for her. His plan was one that stretched over the coming century. It went beyond his death. That house was the very centre of all his dreams. She was only the centre of his broader plan.

Chudalamuttu wished to make all that clear then and there. But even the way he began was wrong. He had not said it in the way he should have, nor had she understood it in the way she should. Thinking he must tell her everything, Chudalamuttu said, 'It's not for you that I'm buying the house.' She could not follow him. He said that together they had a great deal to do. He needed a partner. The house would not even be his. 'The house must grow into a big mansion.'

She smiled. Chudalamuttu continued, 'It is not for either of us.'

'Then who is it for?'

'For the children.'

It seems to Chudalamuttu that she understands nothing of what he is saying. Yet, though the scavenger is not aware of this, she has in fact understood all of it.

The people who walked along the road holding their noses paid no attention to the love scene being enacted underneath the mango tree. A love scene in a night-soil depot? And at midday, too. When the son of a rich man meets a rich man's daughter it is in a moonlit garden – that's the setting in which it is supposed to take place. A man is asking a woman to join him in setting up a family. The excitement when two hearts meet is to be found even here. With all the beating and throbbing of Chudalamuttu's heart he is not able to say all he wants to say.

In the distance two hand-carts could be seen approaching. Valli and Chudalamuttu went to their respective carts. They worked with redoubled strength and energy. To all appearances nothing had happened between them.

Valli and Chudalamuttu were married. Among the scavengers it was a very special occasion. Everyone said she was a lucky woman.

While she was still a child Valli's parents had died. After that the only relative she had in the world was a sister of her father's. It was she who had adopted her and brought her up. The occupation by which she earned her living on a regular basis was as a sweeper in Alleppey town, though once in a while she would do the temporary job of scavenger. Now and again Valli would help her aunt.

On the very day the marriage took place they moved to the old hut in Chudalamuttu's scavenger colony. They redecorated the hut a bit and did all the repairs that were needed. Round the sides they hung bamboo mats. With its concrete floor, the house was unique among scavenger houses. So it was an improved house to which Chudalamuttu brought his wife.

Everything a house needs was there. There were copper pots for cooking, brass water pots, cups, bedsteads, boxes for storing things. In a corner of the room was a picture of Lord Muruga, the most popular Hindu deity in South India, and this was decorated with garlands.

Valli was filled with pride. Not only there, but also in the scavenger colony near the beach where she had been brought up, there was no house as fine as this. Her husband was not without money; he commanded respect.

At nightfall that day he suggested she put a small upright lamp in front of the picture, fill it with oil, make a wick and light it. This she did. While from the other huts came the sound of children weeping, of adults fighting and swearing, in this one, husband and wife were sitting cross-legged in an attitude of prayer. Chudalamuttu said to his wife, 'Please repeat what I say. When praying you must think only of God.'

It was then that Valli said a prayer for the first time. For a long time she looked at her husband as he sat there with legs crossed, eyes closed and the palms of his hands together. From where had he learnt all this? He repeated a verse in praise of God. She tried to say it after him and made mistakes in many places. He corrected her.

When, after the prayers were over, she heard quarrelling and weeping in a neighbouring house, she asked, 'Is someone being beaten? Please go and see.'

'What for?'

'What if he beats her to death?'

'Let him. It's bad enough just living next door to such creatures. We should go somewhere else.'

'Where can we go? It's like this at the beach too.'

'That's not what I mean. We should go to another place where we can have good people as neighbours.'

Valli doubted whether a scavenger could live in a place where scavengers did not usually live. Would decent people tolerate them as neighbours? Then Chudalamuttu asked, 'Must we be satisfied to live for ever as scavengers?'

She did not understand what he was getting at. Is not a scavenger a scavenger? Is it possible to become something else?

That night Chudalamuttu told his wife about all his plans. Great things have to be accomplished. Ways of bettering themselves step by step. She listened to it all. When Chudalamuttu said, 'While I am at work I am studying what the supervisors do, seeing how things'll be if I, too, better myself,' she asked, 'How can we become like those we work under?'

'Just wait and see. But there's one thing you have to remember. We've no time to enjoy ourselves. Only ten days.'

'And then?'

'Then we can't think of enjoying ourselves. We must work hard.'

Valli thought for a little while and then said, 'Even if we work hard we shall be happy as long as we love each other.'

That was what she believed. That was her idea of happiness. It was enough, if they loved each other, to be happy. Chudalamuttu did not understand, for his idea of happiness was something quite different. So he said, 'No, Valli, we shan't be able to live happily. We must work till we die.'

Innocently Valli asked, 'What of that? We must work. So what?'

'If we do, our children will live in comfort.'

She knew that people worked in order to live. Work did not seem to her to be a cause of unhappiness. One cannot live without working. Children have to be brought up. For their sake, a mother and father must endure some suffering and make sacrifices. But even so, how could he say that they would not be happy?

Wondering how they would bring up their children and give them a better station in life, she said, 'Our children must not become scavengers.' Would the children become people of note as her husband said? Valli had her doubts.

Chudalamuttu had taken ten days' leave. He had a reason for it and he asked, 'Would you like to see the country?'

She said she would, and he made clear what he meant when he said they could enjoy themselves for ten days only. During the ten days' leave they would travel around the country and enjoy life; they would be happy. On the eleventh day they would come back and from then on work hard for their children. He made all the preparations necessary to celebrate their honeymoon.

At the end of their ten-day honeymoon Chudalamuttu and Valli returned home.

She had seen so many things! She had had so many wonderful experiences! A new world had opened up before her eyes – a world of marvellous sights! She had seen so many places. A scavenger's tongue could taste. A scavenger's nose could differentiate smells. A scavenger's skin had a sense of touch. If he heard pleasant sounds he could distinguish them. Now she was able to give an account of these revelations, with the wives of Pichandi and Vadivelu as her audience.

The evening she had spent near the Ernakulam lagoon, wearing a silk sari and with flowers in her hair, was a new sort of experience. She decided to spend an evening like that on Alleppey beach too, for she wanted to know if it would be equally enjoyable. But the *dhobi* had taken back the sari she had worn on that day. She would get it from him again.

They would talk of all the interesting things they saw, when on a moonlit night she went with her husband in a small boat which rocked on the waves. Would she be able to enjoy herself again as she had then? No, they agreed, in a lifetime one can have but a week of happiness.

She wanted to relate all her experiences to her friends. But he had ruled that from now on she must not go and see any of them, nor be on intimate terms with them. She was beginning to understand the dirt and filth in a scavenger's life.

Chudalamuttu made all things clear to her. But when he said she must not have anything to do with them – then with whom could she have contact? Was she to live in isolation? She was not even allowed to have dealings with her next-door neighbours!

When the excitement of her new life had worn off and she found herself idle, with nothing to do and no one to talk to, Valli constantly thought about her husband's plans. Could all these things be achieved? To her it all seemed unreal. These were impossible dreams. Throughout that week she had forgotten she was a scavenger. It came as a shock to her the day she realised she would have to come back to being a scavenger. Perhaps her foothold in her new life was not firm enough. Whenever she walked around nicely dressed, or smiled, or went to the cinema, she was uneasy and afraid that someone would reprimand her. They were walking on paths they were not supposed to tread. That did not alter the fact that she and her husband were scavengers. Suppose a scavenger has nothing to do with scavengers, then with whom will he associate?

It was three weeks since Valli had seen the aunt who had brought her up from the time when she was one year old; what expectations that poor old woman had had! She had been waiting, thinking that her adopted daughter would come today or tomorrow. Bringing her up had not even brought her the benefit of having enough betel nuts to chew. The old woman had thought that, when Valli grew up and someone married her, all her own troubles would be over. The poor old thing was still sweeping roads. Even supposing the young woman decided she would like to have her aunt living with them, this was not a request that would be granted.

One day, because she had been waiting in vain in the hope of seeing her, the old woman stopped work early and went to where Valli lived. She took two small cakes with her. When she saw Valli she could not believe it was her foster child. What she saw was an attractive young woman, nicely dressed, her hair combed and plaited, a red mark on her forehead! The old woman felt happy; she had what she wished for from life. But Valli's heart ached. Her aunt had become very thin and worn.

When the old woman said she had been waiting, thinking she would come, Valli's heart burned. There was no reason she could give. She had another fear — that her husband would be cross because her aunt had come to the house.

Valli gave her aunt an oil-bath; she found a good cloth for her to wear; she gave her a meal. She recounted all her travels. Her husband has money; when he has more, he will buy a house and compound. The president has undertaken to buy it for him. Never had the old woman heard words more pleasant to her ears than these.

When she saw Chudalamuttu approaching in the distance Valli went out to meet him. In an apologetic tone of voice she said, 'Auntie has come. As soon as she arrived I gave her a bath.' Chudalamuttu merely gave a bit of a grunt, and Valli went on, 'When I was only a year old my mother and father died. It was she who took me in and cared for me. She has nobody but me.'

In a harsh voice Chudalamuttu asked, 'So what?'

'Nothing. Just don't say anything to her.'

He agreed not to. With a pleasant smile on her face the old woman came out to meet them. Tenderly she complained, 'Dear boy, you haven't even come over to my place.'

'Oh! We weren't able to come.'

Chudalamuttu smiled a little. There was a hint of pride in the smile. Then he went to take a bath. The coldness of Chudalamuttu's behaviour did not touch the old woman.

Chudalamuttu came out, after taking a little longer than usual to have his bath. After dinner it seemed he had to go somewhere. He asked Valli, 'Isn't your aunt going?'

'If she's not . . .' She stopped in the middle of what she was going to say and looked at her husband's face. She wished Chudalamuttu would say definitely that the aunt must leave. But he said nothing.

While they were standing there like that, the old woman came up. It was time for her to go. 'My boy, I've a couple of miles to walk. I must go.'

'In that case, I suppose you must.' How quickly, without any hesitation, he let her take her leave.

That day, for the first time, Chudalamuttu saw Valli's eyes fill with tears.

'My boy, send Valli over to my place after a day or two.'

'It's not possible.'

An unambiguous reply. The harshness with which he said it made even him a little uneasy.

The old woman's face fell. As though she had been at fault, she said, 'No, no. I just said it for no reason. If I take her, who will there be here?'

Valli went with the old woman for a short distance. After they parted Valli stood watching her with tears in her eyes.

In her new home Valli experienced a lack of freedom that she was unable to put her finger on. It was not the sweetheart who spoke to her where the roads met, asked for her love at the depot and who had caused her womanhood to blossom, whom she now saw, but a husband. There was no change in his outward appearance. His body is still strong. Even now he has his crop of wavy hair. There is manliness in his face. But these are not the only things a woman needs.

He makes out that she is not clean enough! As she sees it, he is simply finding fault for its own sake. She sweeps the house and keeps it clean. She bathes regularly. She is clean in every way. Where is there any lack of cleanliness? So Valli is tired of hearing all this criticism. How can she be cleaner and tidier than she is? Chudalamuttu has no positive suggestion to make on the subject of cleanliness. She just cannot understand his way of thinking.

There is another thing: it seems she is a spendthrift! That, too, Valli cannot understand. Although they have money she never handles it. She herself never spends a single paisa. She never strays the slightest fraction from what her husband says. Yet she is a spendthrift!

Valli never goes out of her hut; she is not on close terms with any of the women. She is carrying out to the very letter her husband's instructions not to associate with them. Often she finds this life unbearable. Nevertheless she gives in to him.

People round about think she is very haughty. Nobody cares for her. Yet in her husband's eyes she is full of faults. If some woman says something to her can she not make some sort of reply? One day, grating his teeth in anger, Chudalamuttu said that she would never improve. Valli wept and wept.

The next thing is that she is not devout enough! She tries to become more Godfearing. She knows a lot of hymns and devotional songs. Every day she prays with her husband. Yet in this, too, she does not come up to scratch.

Generally Chudalamuttu does not reprove her. He does not show anger towards her. Yet she is afraid. If someone is always giving orders – how can a woman tolerate his taking away her freedom? Is it not even worse than scolding and beating? How unpleasant it is if everything she does is wrong, and nothing is right.

Every day Chudalamuttu comes back having learnt something new from his superiors. He tries to apply it to his own life. She does not understand his thoughts and his intentions. As a result many things do not happen as he intends.

With so many weighty matters on his mind, Chudalamuttu has no time to sit and talk to his wife. Can a young wife bear this? What Chudalamuttu had said about only being able to enjoy life for ten days now began to make sense to Valli. She had been really happy those ten days. Afterwards they never had a pleasant chat. It is not that her husband cannot talk entertainingly. Yet even though they are young they are getting no fun out of life.

All the time her husband is making calculations and his blood lacks the fire of youth. His embrace does not leave her breathless. His kiss is just for form's sake. As a lover he was more inspiring; when he became a husband he changed; the source of his emotions dried up.

What Chudalamuttu needed was a partner for his life's plans. That he had got.

As she becomes increasingly dissatisfied his wife becomes more and more doubtful about her husband's plans. He is not going to buy a house and compound, to give the house an upper floor, to make it into a mansion. A scavenger cannot become a foreman. How will their children grow up? How will they learn to write? Whatever happens they will still be scavengers. They can only live as scavengers. Nothing will come of all that he has planned.

It seemed to her that all his praying was an act. Sometimes she did not even believe in his love.

Valli put up with it; she compromised. In that way life dragged on. Everything she had wanted was there. Often, not understanding things, she was on the verge of asking questions. But she did not have the courage to ask; she was afraid.

She has never seen a husband–wife relationship like theirs; it is outside her field of experience. The wife has no voice in anything, no authority. The wife obeys the husband; she stands in awe of him. Yet there is no fear like this anywhere else. In scavengers' houses husband and wife will fight; they will exchange blows. Yet she has seen nothing like this anywhere. At times she is not even allowed to talk.

Maybe this is the way things happen in supervisors' houses. This is what love means to them. They make the wife a slave.

In a scavenger's hut very late one night neither husband nor wife has gone to sleep. Neither of them can sleep. Except for the sound of their turning over now and again, all is silent. Neither is talking. Neither has anything to say.

In Chudalamuttu's case many hours usually pass each night without sleep. He has things to think about. For people who have things on their minds deep sleep is impossible.

On this occasion Valli broke the silence: 'Do you think marrying me was a mistake?' She had the impression that Chudalamuttu was quite taken aback.

As if he did not understand the question, he said 'Eh?' to get her to repeat it. Not only was Chudalamuttu's train of thought interrupted, it was all confused; he had to reply to a question he could not answer.

Valli repeated the question: 'What I was asking was, because you married me do you feel you can't do what you planned?'

'I don't feel that.'

When he had given this reply Chudalamuttu felt that it was

inadequate; it was not the right answer. But, because Chudala-muttu's thoughts on that topic were all mixed up, it was not clear to him what answer he ought to give.

Valli went on to ask, 'Sometimes you feel you should have married another woman, don't you?'

'How did you know that?'

'Why do you ask? It's true, isn't it?'

Once again Chudalamuttu was confused. Her questions were dangerous ones; he had not even imagined that such questions could come from her. Yet, as if to rescue him from his state of confusion, a question came to his lips: 'Do you feel that I don't love you?'

Valli answered sharply: 'I feel no such thing.'

'Then why do you put such questions?' Chudalamuttu felt he now had a grip on the situation.

'It's not like that. What I wanted to know was, do you feel you could have got somebody with more money, somebody cleaner and more dignified?'

After a minute or so Chudalamuttu said, 'If I could have got somebody like that, it would have been better.'

Can a wife hear such an answer without getting angry? For a husband to admit such a thing – that he thinks it would have been good if he had got someone better, and that he wishes he had done so! How could she not be expected to get angry? That day, for the first time, she became conscious of her ability to stand up to him: she had a lot to ask; a lot to say. Now she had a full understanding of the situation. She could defy him.

Harshly Valli asked, 'But do you have anybody like that in mind?'

'Did I say that?'

'If you have, just you go and bring her here!'

From then on Valli stood up to him. She strengthened her position. She gave her husband warning. He had courted her for a long time; he had made many promises. She told him, 'I remember it all, everything. I have not forgotten a single word you said. Just you let me down: I'll show you!'

That was a terrible threat. She went on: 'You put a *tali* round my neck as a sign of marriage – where are you keeping her?' Thus she affirmed her rights as the one he had taken as his wife.

'No matter what, she's bound to be a scavenger's daughter. Where is she?'

Chudalamuttu was caught in a dangerous position. He had not forgotten those times when he was attracted by her, when he thought only of her; he could never forget. He had seen her as the realisation of all his life's dreams. He had not been able to stand before her without his legs shaking, nor speak to her without stammering. What she said was true. He had promised her a love that would endure.

Yet does not a man who has plans and ambitions in life feel once in a while that things could have been better if he had taken as his wife a girl who was superior to the one he has married? Is it inconsistent with love? Does it mean he renounces her?

Valli went on asking, 'Where is she, where is she?' She further accused him of not talking nicely to her: because he has another girl, he is always thinking of her. Valli's attack was violent and unstoppable. She wept. She waved her arms. It was almost as if she was going mad.

Chudalamuttu did not know what to do. How was he to console her? How was he to silence the doubt that had entered her mind? If he did not, all his dreams would be shattered. Until then Chudalamuttu had not realised how essential she was in his life.

Chudalamuttu was defeated; utterly defeated. Things had reached the stage where he had to admit that she was essential to him. So she understood where his weakness lay.

Smallpox

There had never been such a long, hot summer. For months it had not rained. In the sweltering heat all living things wilted. It was a state of affairs that presaged an attack by some infectious disease or other.

That is exactly what happened: smallpox! And smallpox of a particularly virulent kind. It never goes beyond six or eight days, and it is fatal. Hardly anyone who gets it can be expected to survive.

Everyone was aware of the situation. People panicked. But even so, trade went on. Factories were working. The streets were full of people. No one knew where the outbreaks were.

Everyone began to ask what the municipality was doing. No one could say whether they were doing anything or not. Some vaccinators were running around. That was all. Apart from that no one knew whether any action was being taken. In the nearby Kattanad District and in one part of Shertala Taluk the disease began to spread.

All in all the situation was reaching the point that gives rise to panic. A rumour spread that the town's cinemas were to have their licences revoked. Night-time entertainments were no longer permitted. Certain factories might be closed for some time. It was rumoured that those were the factories where there was a high incidence of the disease. The matter would be discussed at the next meeting of the municipal council. A council member had submitted a resolution.

The rumours only served to make the cinema proprietors and the factory managers go to the houses of council members, of the municipal president, of the chairman of the municipal department of health. At the next council meeting the report of the chairman of the health department was read out. By means of statistics he proved that there was no justification for saying that all that much of a state of panic had developed in the town. Over a period of a month nine cases of smallpox had been reported. Only two had proved fatal. For ten days no new cases had been reported. Such was the tenor of his report. On the basis of this report the resolution that had been submitted for the consideration of the council was withdrawn. The council president was, however, given authority to appoint four more vaccinators.

Meanwhile the president found himself faced with another problem. There was also smallpox in all the houses near where he lived. And in some places death had ensued. After sending his wife and children to Trivandrum he locked up his house and went to live somewhere else for the time being. All this was only a temporary inconvenience. It was not this which bothered him. Daily the number of sweepers and scavangers from the area near the seashore was getting smaller. For the time being Keshava Pillai was getting others to do the work. But if things went on like this it would not be possible to fill the gap even in that way. The president and the overseer gave the matter careful thought, and the president asked the latter, 'Is it only by the seashore, Keshava Pillai?'

'No one has got it at the northern end of the town yet, sir.'

'But they can catch it at any time. And if they do catch it, weak and filthy as they are, there'll not be a single one left.'

Keshava Pillai agreed. Twenty years earlier there had been a similar outbreak. On that occasion there had not been one survivor. Within a fortnight there had not been a single scavenger left in town. At that time, too, Keshava Pillai had been overseer. Curious, the president asked, 'What did you do that time, Keshava Pillai?'

'It is enough that I got it done. Even now, when I think of it, I wonder how I managed it. We had to spent a lot of money.'

'Was there a day when the work was not done?'

'No. I saw to it that that didn't happen.'

'How did you manage it?'

'At the start of the epidemic I went with some money to Tirunelveli. There I made arrangements to bring back some replacements. Within a week of my return here, none of the old lot were left.'

The president reflected for a while and then asked, 'Do we need to go to Tirunelveli this time as well?' Keshava Pillai did not reply at once. The president went on, 'If we do not do what is necessary early enough, and then things get into a mess . . . .?'

Keshava Pillai replied, 'I've been thinking about that too. I kept wanting to tell you.'

'Roughly how much money do you need?'

'Last time I took two thousand rupees. It's very difficult to get these people. They need money for the trip. It's very difficult. If they know we need them, they drive a hard bargain.'

'Still, you'd better go.'

Keshava Pillai agreed. The president had a further suggestion to make: 'There's something you must do tomorrow. You should take a vaccinator and have all those who live in the northern section immunised. For the work must go on at least till you get back, mustn't it? What if they all kick the bucket before then?'

In the light of his experience, Keshava Pillai opposed the idea. 'No, we shouldn't do that. It's even riskier. If they are vaccinated they get a temperature. If they get a temperature the work doesn't get done. In some cases it might even happen that they get the disease precisely because they've been vaccinated.'

This seemed like good sense to the president. Keshava Pillai went on in a subdued tone: 'There's another thing. I've been thinking about it for a while. It's high time we changed all these people. We shouldn't keep them on more than ten years. What's more, this is a good time. Though the union broke up, even now all the talk is about a union. They're still out to start a union. It's difficult to get them to do their job. This is a good opportunity.'

The president did not grasp the meaning of his last sentence. He asked, 'In what way?'

Keshava Pillai hummed and hawed a bit and then said, 'It won't be a case of sacking them.'

'Let them die. That's it, isn't it? Fine!' The president laughed at what seemed to him the funny side of this. Keshava Pillai, too, smiled.

'Very good, Keshava Pillai, very good!'

'It's not that, sir. I've been among these creatures in this municipality for many years. When they've been worn down like this over a period of ten or fifteen years we need to get new men. Then the work will get done.'

The president agreed that this was so. Yet deep down there was a touch of uneasiness, which showed when he asked, 'Aren't they men too? Don't they have children and infants, Keshava Pillai?'

With an expression of amazement, Keshava Pillai asked, 'Are they men too? Fine!'

The president also found that remark a bit of a joke. Anyway, after telling him to do what was necessary, he dismissed Keshava Pillai. The president realised that Keshava Pillai was the town council's most useful official. But the management of the town council would be very difficult.

In all the temples of the town and the surrounding parts night has become day. These days the entrance gates are virtually never closed. For a whole month, offerings have been made. Tuesdays and Fridays being popularly believed to be especially bad days for smallpox, bribes have been offered to the temple officials to gain entry on those days. Moreover, the offerings are not on a small scale. How many well-to-do people there are in Alleppey! Each day one hears that today such-and-such a rich man is doing *pooja*. An effort is made every day to improve on the offerings that have been made earlier. To judge from the competition, one would think that everyone was trying to increase his own renown! Perhaps that is indeed the motivation. This apart, will not their business prosper too?

This sort of thing is happening not only in the Hindu temples, but also in Christian churches, in accordance with the practices of each religion. Upper-class Christians have even had offerings made in Hindu temples, and upper-class Hindus have had masses said in Christian churches. At night-time Muslims go without sleep to say prayers aloud in the streets, their traditional fires burning in the earthen pots.

People stand around aimlessly. What can be done to escape this danger? They make offerings of flowers; or they say mass. In superstition religions have come together. So a Christian puts his trust in flower offerings, and a Hindu puts his in mass. When he hears the prayers chanted in the streets by Muslims the frightened Hindu feels comforted.

The municipal president's offering does not consist simply of flowers; on that day there is animal sacrifice and *Durga pooja* too. Offerings are being made not only in Mullaikkal, but also in Pazhavidu, Kidangamparambam and Kottankulangara. They are even being made in Pazhayanadippalli! It is a special day in the town. Wishing to join in, the scavengers decide on a contribution of three rupees each.

The ceremonies passed. But no matter what had taken place, the danger had not lessened. Among the scavengers living by the seashore the number of deaths was increasing. Fear grew among those in the northern part of the town. What remedy could there be?

Under the leadership of Chudalamuttu all the scavengers got together to discuss the situation. Everyone agreed with Chudalamuttu that they would be saved from this peril through faith in God. They should make offerings in order to obtain God's mercy. No one had anything against that. So they decided that there should be special offerings in the temple and in churches in the name of the scavengers. Chudalamuttu was to take responsibility for this; the overseer would arrange for it to be done.

Within two or three days the money was collected. Never before had anything happened like this, without argument. The next day the money had to be handed over to the overseer. In the evening, when Chudalamuttu was checking through the contributions, Valli, who was standing watching, asked, 'Did they all give something?'

Chudalamuttu mumbled something in reply.

'Did you put something in for us too?'

Chudalamuttu merely gave a sort of grunt. Valli felt a bit doubtful. Gradually she was getting to know him. Their share was not included; she had a feeling he had not put it in. However she did not come out with it directly. After a while she said, 'Up by the seashore there's an old woman, my aunt. She has no one. Something should be put in for her.'

Valli had spoken in an authoritative tone. Unintentionally so. It just came out like that. Three more rupees to be spent! Chudalamuttu looked up and asked, 'Why?'

'You ask why? Why are we doing all this?'

Chudalamuttu had no further answer. Saying he had nothing on him, he put all the money in a piece of cloth and tied it up.

Valli could not bear it. She could not help crying. Not because of the denial of her wishes, but because the old woman lived alone in a quarter where two or three were dying every day. And no contribution towards the offering had been made for her.

There was a lot she wanted to say. She tried to get close to him. But for a long time she could not get near him. She asked him: 'How much do you plan to make out of this?'

It was a completely unexpected question – particularly from her. When he was counting the money, maybe he had been making some sort of calculation. Whatever the case, it was not possible to say for sure that his thoughts were not the least dishonourable. Though he could have used his authority and silenced her by scolding, he said, 'This offering is being made for us as a group, isn't it? So what does it matter if her money is not included? But if you want, I'll put that in, too, tomorrow.'

So for the time being the disagreement between husband and wife came to an end. Valli had won. As a result of that victory all her suppressed desires raised their heads. The old woman was living there alone. What if she said they should bring her here? Why not let her live here for the time being? That was a duty she owed to her aunt; was she not entitled to ask that she be allowed to stay with them?

Meanwhile Chudalamuttu's thoughts were working in another direction. She is getting in his way. She is asking inconvenient questions. In her eyes he has become small; more than that, she has made him small. She knows nothing about his schemes. Will it all work out or not?

While such thoughts were passing through his mind, she demanded, 'Until this epidemic is over, we must bring Auntie here to stay.'

Oh hell! That very possibility had crossed Chudalamuttu's mind. If the old woman stayed by the seashore, and in the present hazard were to pass away, then so be it. That was how his thoughts had been running. And now his wife comes up with this demand. Chudalamuttu undertook to have the aunt sent for. So yet another victory was won. Valli was relieved.

The next day, when he came back from work, Chudalamuttu said to his wife, 'Your auntie is running a temperature.'

Sundiran's wife got a temperature. The fever worsened and one Tuesday spots appeared all over her body.

So the disease spread to that quarter too. Chudalamuttu was very uneasy. Either they must go and live away from there; or they must get the sick woman moved. It was not convenient for Chudalamuttu suddenly to move from there.

All the scavengers, including Chudalamuttu, met in Pichandi's house. They had also arranged for a man who knew about the disease to come. After he had seen the sick woman he joined them.

The expert gave his frank opinion: 'This illness is not a trivial matter; it is not yet possible to make out what sort of spots they are. Until three or four days have gone by, we can't say what form of the disease she's got.'

Sundiran burst out crying. He had married her when she was twelve years old. Even though they were perpetually fighting each other, she was a loving woman. Not once had she failed to cook him a meal. If Sundiran did not have money to go to the toddy shop she would somehow find some for him. He had a lot of things like this to say. If the truth were told, he felt it very deeply. Round him were five children. The eldest was only eight. Helplessly he asked, 'What am I to do with these poor things?'

Then the expert stated, 'We can't say she's likely to die. To judge from her present state the spots will be the less dangerous white sort. But it might also develop into the black sort. Anyhow, we must take precautions.'

Sundiran prayed that this might not happen. For what else was there for him to do?

Next they went into the treatment of the sick woman. The expert explained that if they used herbal remedies they would need at least fifty rupees. They would need to get two people from somewhere to look after the patient. And they would need a doctor. 'That's the least it will cost; the very least. Work it out for yourself. What will the expenditure come to for three people, including the patient? Then add the cost of medicine and so on.'

Chudalamuttu intervened, 'Herbal treatment's no good.

Particularly not for this. If you want something that'll work you have to spend money. Do you have any?'

Sundiran threw out his hands and looked heavenwards with tears in his eyes. 'Almighty God! I haven't a single paisa.'

His sad cry touched everyone's heart. Chudalamuttu understood. Before anyone could say anything, he explained how he saw it: 'It seems to me that we should send her to hospital. That's the best thing.'

Impatiently Chudalamuttu waited for an answer. He doubted whether this view would be acceptable. Sundiran's pitiable state had touched everyone so much.

Shuppu opposed the idea. He spoke with a hint of antagonism in his voice: 'In that case, why don't you kill her now?'

Chudalamuttu retorted, 'Is it for this that the government has spent money on building hospitals? Do you think people die just because they are put in hospitals?'

Vadivelu agreed with Shuppu: 'If you've got money the hospital's fine. If not – then that's the way it is.'

Chudalamuttu felt that his reasoning was not all that illogical. To refute what they had said he tried another tack: 'If you don't have any more time to live, wherever you are you'll die. The only thing is that it'll be a consolation if you get your illness checked by someone who knows what's what.'

'That's not how it is,' said Vadivelu. 'Even without coming to the end of their life people die.'

'How can that be?' asked Chudalamuttu.

Whilst they were arguing in this way, Palani said that in his view local medicine was good for this sickness. Sundiran sat there with nothing to say. He just wept. The children pressed around him. One was sleeping with its head on his lap. He would do whatever his friends wished. Apart from them he had no one.

'Good, but is there any money for this sort of medicine?' asked Chudalamuttu.

For some time no one spoke. They already knew that Sundiran had none. Shuppu broke the silence: 'There are twenty families here. Each must give two rupees. That's how we should arrange for the treatment. For he's one of us, isn't he?'

Vadivelu gave his support. All who were present supported the proposal. Only Chudalamuttu said nothing. So the meeting brightened up a bit, for they saw a way out. They all said they would give the money the following day. With the serious expression that goes with an important announcement, Chudalamuttu asked, 'Do you know that this is catching?'

Shuppu's emphatic rejoinder was, 'We know; we're well aware of it.'

'But if we keep her here, it will spread. Then who will supply the money that will be needed?'

Shuppu got angry. 'They're all going to die! Isn't it the case that every five or six years there's an outbreak of cholera or typhoid or something that kills off everybody in this sort of group?'

It was clear to Chudalamuttu that no one was going to go along with him. For a while he was silent. Then he said, 'I shan't give a paisa.'

One man exploded with the question: 'Suppose we don't want your money?'

Another man said, 'Not only that, we won't take your money for this. We know you. It was you who broke up our union. Just look at these children. And you thought you could send their mother to the hospital and kill her off there! You, with your heart of stone, who the hell are you? Are you human?'

Chudalamuttu left in a huff. The defeat had unsettled him.

Anxiously Valli asked what had happened. Chudalamuttu said, 'They're going to leave her here and ruin the place.'

Valli did not understand. He explained that if they did not send her to the hospital the disease would spread. She said that if they sent the sick woman to the hospital she would die. She felt sorry for the children who were going to be orphaned.

Chudalamuttu kept back what he thought about all this, for he was afraid of her. But he had made up his mind about what he would do.

It was a heart-rending scene. The sick woman pleaded with them not to be sent to hospital. She believed that if she entered the hospital she would die. No one need worry about her at all; she would just lie on her bed. If she was going to die, then so be it – this was how she felt.

The scavengers were all standing around helplessly. It was the president who had ordered that she be moved to the hospital, on the grounds that a smallpox patient should not be kept in a densely populated area. So the bearers had come with a stretcher. What were her friends to do? The previous day they had decided to take a collection and have somebody brought in to look after her; some money had been collected. But what was the use? Sundiran lay there crying as if the mother of his children was going to her death. In their loneliness the children clustered round him. All they knew was that something momentous was happening. Sadly they watched it all.

When the bearers lifted her on to the stretcher she cried out, and not just because of the physical pain. It was the agony of the anticipation of approaching death. They were going to separate her from all that she loved. And she called out, 'Just leave me here. That's all I want.'

Sundiran heard her. He felt as if they were taking her off to the cremation ground. He jumped up to look at her for the last time. The others held him back. Then she begged them: 'Let me have a look at my children!' Sundiran asked that her request be granted. But no; it is not good to accede to such a request. The disease is smallpox.

When they had picked her up and were going away from the hut one of her children saw what was happening. Was it not two days since he had seen his mother? He called out, 'Father! Mother!'

The other children saw it too. One of the younger ones began to scream after its mother. It tried to free itself from Sundiran, who was carrying it on his hip. The next eldest child was crying. The eldest asked, 'Where are they taking her, Father?'

No one replied. Then the mother called out to one of the children by name. They all watched her being carried away. Heartbroken, Sundiran called out in a loud voice: 'Ammu!' From the distance came the reply: 'Husband!' Watching that tragic journey they all sighed.

Chudalamuttu and Valli stood in front of their hut watching. Valli was weeping. When they had got a good way off with Ammu, Chudalamuttu felt relieved.

'Phew! That's one danger out of the way.'

His unfeeling comment pierced Valli's heart. The force of her

reaction was beyond her control. Seething with anger she said,
'You louse!'

Chudalamuttu was rather scared as Valli went on: 'After killing
the mother and leaving those five poor children with nobody
to . . .' She could not say the rest of it. She felt that this was
another of those things that were building a barrier between them.

After a short while Chudalamuttu said, 'That's fate.'

'Fate! Then why do you sit with your eyes closed before the
image of God and pray?'

Chudalamuttu managed to retrieve his sense of authority: 'Go!
Go inside!'

She went in.

Though it was in order to remove the danger to the scavenger
colony that Chudalamuttu had used his influence with the
municipality to have Sundiran's wife taken to hospital to die, the
danger was still with them. The next day a scavenger called
Virabahu had fever. After that Vadivelu's wife got it. So, within
the space of a week, more than twenty people in the scavenger
colony caught smallpox. Almost all were serious cases.

Chudalamuttu started looking for another house.

Sundiran's eldest child was to be seen walking along the road
carrying the youngest one on his hip. The other three followed
behind. After a few days there were only four children. A few more
days later the eldest one no longer had a burden to carry on his
hip. Those who remained were split up in different parts of the
town. The remnants of that broken family could be seen hanging
about in front of shops or by the roadside.

Nobody knows how many people died in that smallpox outbreak or how many survived. However Keshava Pillai saved the
town. He and Chudalamuttu went together and brought some
men from Tirunelveli. They were good workers. What did it
matter if it cost the municipality a little more money?

Betrayal

A moonlit night in the scavenger colony next to the night-soil depot. On the open space in front of the huts the scavengers are sitting round a pot containing toddy. Of those we have already met there is only one man remaining. Just Pichandi! All the rest are new men.

It is the day after they draw their pay. Cooking fires are burning in all the huts; the children are howling; the mothers are scolding them – all told there is quite a racket. Though the faces have changed, there is no noticeable difference. For the new ones who take over it is quite a saving to have these huts ready and waiting. The pattern of life for this class of people is for one contagious disease or another to come along every two or three years to annihilate them.

They are telling one another about the amounts they have drawn. This time Palaniyandi got twelve rupees. The previous month he had learnt that his wages were eighteen rupees. Muniswami asked him: 'How on earth did you find that out?'

'The overseer told me.' They all thought in that case it must be a lie.

Then someone else said, 'The pay is the same for all of us. The same as for the navvies and sweepers.'

This was another point on which they were not able to agree. Nevertheless they did not get involved in a heated argument about it. Why should they? What did it matter how many rupees were due to them each month? They would not get that amount. Thus the conversation went on, and they came to what they had given Chudalamuttu the previous day. Muniswami had given seven rupees, Palaniyandi six, Vallinayagam eight – and so on.

One man said, 'Fine, so how many rupees all told has he got from us this time?'

Another man tried to work it out. Each one said what he had given. Soon the calculation went wrong. He added it up again. It came to eighty rupees. Then somebody else spoke, 'He must have got some from the beach lot also.'

Yet another man had something else he wanted to know: 'If we borrow five rupees today how much do we have to give back?'

For the five rupees he had borrowed, Muniswami had given back seven. It was a fortnight earlier that he had borrowed it. So each one told of the debts he had incurred and how much he had paid back. Like one who was in the know as regards these transactions, Vallinayagam said, 'But half of what he makes goes to the overseer. He's the one who holds it, isn't he?'

'Anyway,' said someone else, 'our friend must make some money out of the deal.'

Pichandi, who had remained silent for a while, now joined in the discussion. 'He does. And it's not small change he's getting, but real money. That's the way a man who doesn't drink toddy and so on betters himself. He's going to buy a house and compound.'

'Why has he gone to live away from us?' asked Vallinayagam.

'That's the way it is. His kids aren't going to be scavengers.'

Pichandi gave an account of Chudalamuttu's life. He told of Ishukkumuttu's death and of Chudalamuttu's marriage. When he came to the story of the union Pichandi became a little emotional as he said, 'Chudalamuttu is a great friend of mine. He is fond of me too. It couldn't be otherwise. But he's still a traitor. We can't trust him. For the way the louse betrayed us, if I remain an Alleppey scavenger, I'll teach him a lesson. Friendship is one thing; the way people behave towards you is another. That's for sure.'

They were curious to hear the story of the union and Pichandi told it. At the end they said, 'He let everybody down, didn't he?'

'Yes.'

That was a matter on which there was no difference of opinion.

They did not know what their wages should be. Someone was playing a game with them. They may have been drunk but they were conscious of their many grievances of this sort. One man expressed the view that Pichandi, who was very familiar with Alleppey town, was the right person to get a union going.

Pichandi agreed to do it. With great confidence he said, 'I'll set up a union. I know how to go about it. But you must all remember one thing. We must stand firm. There must be no backing down. Chudalamuttu will try to prevent it. That too must be kept in mind.'

Muniswami jumped in: 'Let anybody you like try to stop it. We need a union.'

Yes, they are ready to face any opposition. They need a union.

Pichandi took on the seriousness of a leader. He shook his head. 'Fine, but there's one thing you must do. Even if it means starving to death, don't accept a loan from Chudalamuttu! If you'll agree to that, then I'll see to the union business.'

'That's okay. Shan't we be better off that way?' The proposal was accepted unanimously.

They came to the next item on the agenda. They would have to call a meeting. They fixed a day for it. Pichandi recommended them to keep these matters secret.

So the feeling of getting united grew up once again. Pichandi also became a leader.

However, when the effect of drink wore off, Pichandi became uneasy. He remembered all that he had said about Chudalamuttu. Although it was all true, it was not the sort of thing that should have been said. It would all reach Chudalamuttu's ears. How would he be able to look Chudalamuttu in the face? Pichandi had been his friend; he still was. No one else had found the same genuine happiness in the way Chudalamuttu had improved himself. His going up in the world was a source of pride to Pichandi. Who else had stood by Chudalamuttu in his time of trouble?

It was not that Chudalamuttu had done anything special for him. But Pichandi was his friend. It might seem absurd. Yet are there not plenty of relationships like that – friendships whose roots we cannot find?

There was another thing: he would now have to stand up to Chudalamuttu. Pichandi doubted whether he had the necessary strength. But they absolutely must have a union.

*   *   *

While all this talk was going on in the scavenger colony, Chudalamuttu, in his rented house near Shavakkotta Bridge, had closed all his doors and windows and was checking and counting his money. Valli was sitting near him. When he had worked out how much there was, he began to make a mental calculation, and this took quite a bit of time.

Valli had a lot of questions to ask. She wanted to know how much they had saved altogether; how many rupees they had entrusted to the president; how many rupees would be needed to buy the house and compound – many things of this kind. But if questions are asked when one is counting money and making calculations, the arithmetic goes wrong. Nevertheless a rebellious attitude was taking root in her. Should she not also be made aware of these calculations? Why so much secrecy?

Without letting them jingle together, Chudalamuttu gathered up the coins quietly and put them in a cloth bag. Such avarice! Wasn't she also entitled to a part in this? 'How many rupees have you got there?' she asked.

Her voice seemed a little loud and Chudalamuttu answered, 'Be quiet. Speak softly.'

'What for?'

'Someone will hear.'

'What if they do?'

Chudalamuttu got angry. 'In that case, go and bawl it out to everybody that we've got money here.'

Chudalamuttu put the cloth bag in a box and got up. Valli's rebelliousness had made her very uneasy. She had to ask; she had to know; she had to establish her rights in all of this; but shouldn't he tell her things of this sort without being asked? Should not her rights in such matters be admitted?

As if she were not as bright as he had thought, Chudalamuttu said, 'What we have got so far is not enough. If we are to get the house and compound we need to wait some time longer. How is it to be done? It can only be done if a man's wife isn't lacking in the right sort of qualities.'

'Lacking in what sort of qualities?' Valli asked.

'You're useless, that's what. If you weren't, couldn't you make something out of the money we've got here?'

'Have you ever entrusted any of it to me?'

'Even if I had, it wouldn't have been any use.'

Chudalamuttu began to explain in detail the way to make money grow. All their neighbours were short of money. Loans could be made at a good rate of interest. All they needed to do was to be careful about it. If she, too, were to try this, how quickly they could increase their capital.

Valli listened attentively to all that Chudalamuttu said. But she was unconvinced. More than that, for some reason she could not entirely explain, she felt a sort of anger welling up inside her. When he had finished talking she said, 'If we try to make a killing like that we shan't manage to keep it.'

Not understanding her feeling of anger, Chudalamuttu tried to contradict what she had said.

'Then how do all these well-off people make money?' he asked.

Chudalamuttu then went on to explain how he was learning things. When he went with bucket and shovel into the latrines he was not simply doing the work of a scavenger. He was looking; he was observing things; he was learning. He was blessed with the right sort of intelligence to adapt and apply in his own life the lessons he learnt. A person like that would better himself. But he had one complaint: his wife did not understand all this.

'Why don't I send you out to work? Have you thought of that? If I sent you, we should make more money. Then why not send you? Why do I say that you must keep this house clean? Think about it. I have an object in all this. But you won't try to understand.'

Next Chudalamuttu described the principles on which he based his life. Nothing of what he was doing was for himself; nor was it for her. It was for the next generation; it was for their children's children. They would not be scavengers. He gave her an account of what he had got together so far. He had handed over three hundred rupees to the president for safe-keeping. A part of what he now had in his own possession he was going to give to the president the next day.

Valli's feeling of antagonism was reduced to a certain extent. At least she had come to know this much. Yet it was not enough. Was it not her right to be consulted too? She could not bear the accusation that she lacked the right sort of qualities.

'Suppose the president doesn't return the rupees you have handed over to him?' she asked.

Chudalamuttu was taken aback. What if he didn't return them? If he didn't, what could be done? It was money, wasn't it? Who would not covet it?

For a while Chudalamuttu could hardly breathe. Valli watched his uneasiness. She even enjoyed it a little.

When he had first entrusted money to the president Chudala-muttu had not had so much. He was nothing like so well-off. Valli was bright; she was sharp. Yet would a big man like the president be guilty of such a breach of trust with a scavenger?

That night Chudalamuttu talked of very many things; he discussed them; he showed respect for her opinions. Yet he was not persuaded that she had developed enough to go along with his plans.

So Pichandi had decided to form a union! He had no intention of even consulting Chudalamuttu. The scavengers intended to isolate him. No one wanted anything to do with Chudalamuttu.

Chudalamuttu felt the same way about it. Let them form a union; let them leave him out. But supposing they do not want anything to do with him – Chudalamuttu knows that here they are embarking on something they will find unworkable. Can Alleppey scavengers ever go more than a few days without borrowing money? These arrangements were something that bound the scavengers and Chudalamuttu together.

But Chudalamuttu could not stand aloof from it all. The news that a union was to be formed reached the overseer; the president, too, had heard of it. To whom, apart from Chudalamuttu, could the responsibility be given for smashing this renewed attempt?

Chudalamuttu faced another crisis. Pichandi was the one he had to oppose. On top of that, the scavengers were united. But this argument was not acceptable to the higher authorities.

'What is it to you if you break off with Pichandi?'

When the overseer asked him this Chudalamuttu was caught in a dilemma.

'It's not possible to break off with Pichandi,' he said. 'He's not the sort of man to break off a relationship. He doesn't know how to.'

The overseer could not make head or tail of that. Then Chudalamuttu asked, 'But what if you give Pichandi the sack?'

Chudalamuttu thought this was a good idea. But it did not get the expected reaction. Pichandi was the scavengers' leader now. What if Pichandi was sacked and then everyone went on strike? Wasn't this too much of a risk at a time when the municipality could not afford a strike?

The overseer gave firm instructions that the effort to unite must be brought to nothing.

When he saw Pichandi the next day Chudalamuttu said not a word. In the night-soil depot the day after that, when the scavengers were arguing among themselves as to what made a good latrine, Chudalamuttu deliberately made fun of Pichandi. On the third day a story was going round that Pichandi had spoken ill of Chudalamuttu. That same evening Pichani went to Chudalamuttu's house and saw him. With pain in his heart, Pichandi said, 'I wouldn't say such a thing. I didn't say it. When I feel glad to see how you are bettering yourself . . .'

Chudalamuttu gave Pichandi a good telling-off and told him to get out. When Pichandi went off with tears in his eyes Valli came out and asked, 'What's all this about?' She asked who Pichandi was to Chudalamuttu. And what exactly had he done?

Chudalamuttu could not forget the things that had happened in the past. He remembered it all. There was one man in the whole world who had any affection for him. That was Pichandi. Yet Chudalamuttu needed to break off with Pichandi. But Valli did not understand this. No one understood it.

One day Chudalamuttu went to the night-soil depot with a piece of news. At that time only Palaniyandi was around. Nobody else had arrived. Chudalamuttu was dying to tell someone. It was as if there was something inside him trying to push the news out. For some unknown reason it got stuck in his parched throat. The story he had to tell concerned something serious.

There had not been too many moments in Chudalamuttu's life when his insides had been bursting with the pressure of emotions.

Almost without realising it, he came out with the piece of news to Palaniyandi.

'There was a theft in the Reddiar's house,' he said, adding in a lower voice, 'They say it was Pichandi.'

Palaniyandi went up to Chudalamuttu and asked, 'You mean the theft that took place the other day?'

'Yes.'

Casually Chudalamuttu went on: 'It seems he snatched a chain from a child's neck.'

'Do the police know?'

'They'll have found out. We'd better not say anything.' Chudalamuttu finished his work quickly.

The news spread like wildfire in the scavenger colony. It was Pichandi who had carried out the theft!

Pichandi was weeping and swearing that he was innocent. If they wanted, let them search his house. If he possessed anything as valuable as that, would he be in such a sorry state? How long was it since they had had two square meals a day? In all his forty years Pichandi had never done anything bad like that.

Muniswami said what he thought should be done: 'Suppose you go away from here for a few days?'

They all went along with that idea. The truth will come out in the end, will it not? Meanwhile, would there not be a lot of risks? Pichandi, heartbroken, said, 'What will my children do?'

Vallinayagam consoled him: 'Don't bother yourself about that. We'll look after them. When trouble comes they'll be our children. As long as there's food in the house your children, too, will eat.'

Palaniyandi and Muniswami gave the same undertaking.

'But you must go this very night. Maybe the police will come and make a search.'

Everybody considered this the best course of action.

Then another problem occurred to him. If he went without leave, would he get work when he got back? Muniswami said he would take care of that. He would ask the overseer for leave. But there was one difficulty. If leave was to be sanctioned they would have to give the overseer at least five rupees.

With tears in his eyes Pichandi said, 'I don't have a paisa.'

For a moment they were all silent. Muniswami proposed a solution: 'We must all chip in.'

Muniswami had seven chakrams. Vallinayagam could manage nine chakrams. So they each promised a sum in accordance with their means. There was one more thing: what reason was to be given for asking for time off? The best thing would be to say he was ill.

They all swore by what they held sacred, by what they loved most dearly, that they would never come out with the real reason why Pichandi had taken time off. After entrusting his family to his friends and to God, and after kissing his children, Pichandi left the house to the sounds of weeping and went off.

The next day Vallinayagam and Muniswami told Chudalamuttu about it. It seemed that Chudalamuttu had got the news from a police officer!

'But Pichandi didn't do it,' said Muniswami.

Chudalamuttu smiled meaningfully. 'None of you really knows Pichandi. He could swipe an elephant in broad daylight.'

'If a bloke has money, will he put it away and let his family starve?'

'That's the sign of a smart thief. Thinking it will give the game away, he won't spend it. Anyway it'll all come out in the end.'

Muniswami and Vallinayagam had nothing to say. Perhaps Chudalamuttu was right in what he said. Chudalamuttu continued: 'I wouldn't say something about Pichandi that wasn't true. He's given me a lot of help. But it's clear that he's not the type of fellow who would hesitate to do such a thing.'

'True enough,' said Vallinayagam, 'He must have taken it.'

'Yes,' Muniswami agreed. 'But in that case where's the loot?'

'It must be there,' said Chudalamuttu. 'Unless he's got it on him.'

Muniswami and Vallinayagam engaged in silent thought. Poor, naive creatures! You could make them believe anything. One by one Chudalamuttu began to list the ways in which Pichandi had helped him. Finally he asked, 'Would I spread false rumours about a man like that?'

Muniswami shook his head and said, 'No.'

After they left Chudalamuttu, Muniswami asked Vallinayagam, 'If this is so, why are we helping out his wife and kids?'

Vallinayagam replied, 'That's what I was thinking too.'

Though he had achieved what he wanted, it was not a light-hearted Chudalamuttu who went off. For the present the formation of a union had been held up. Pichandi's influence with the scavengers had been reduced. But the fact remained that Pichandi was a man who had loved him. Was there really and truly a case like that against Pichandi? Or had the overseer only told him so to frighten him? When the news broke it had not even occurred to Chudalamuttu that Pichandi would go away. Now Chudalamuttu was the cause of everything. When Pichandi came back again, how would he look him in the face? What excuse could he give? The whole thing preyed on Chudalamuttu's mind. Apart from that, what if Valli found out about all this – and how could she fail to find out?

Once again the scavengers started to take loans from Chudalamuttu.

The scavengers met near their houses. They had a number of serious matters to consider. Pichandi had committed the theft. His wife was hiding the stolen property. In these circumstances no one was responsible for looking after his family.

Muniswami stated his views forcefully. All agreed that if this was the case there was no necessity to give anything to Pichandi and his children.

Vallinayagam asked, 'What if we fetch his wife and ask her straight out?' Virabahu ran off to Pichandi's hut.

Palaniyandi asked, 'What about Pichandi? Where is he?' No one had any idea.

'How many days' leave did he get?'

'Fifteen.'

'Then he's got to come back on the sixteenth, hasn't he?'

'Yes.'

'But with things as they are, he won't return.'

'If he doesn't come, that's just too bad.'

Pichandi's wife, Alamelu, was brought along for questioning. She was no more than a skeleton dressed in a badly torn sari.

In an authoritative tone Muniswami said, 'Right, woman, tell the truth! Where's the stuff?'

Alamelu had no idea what he was talking about.

'What stuff do you mean?'

Muniswami stuck out his chest. 'Hm. You want to know what stuff? The stuff that was taken from the Reddiar's house.'

Alamelu started to weep.

'What is it, woman? Tell the truth. Pichandi pinched it.'

What was the poor woman to say? Her husband was not the sort of man to do a thing like that. He had not done it. As God in heaven was her witness. But no one believed that witness. Alamelu wept. To try and make it more credible she told them of her difficulties: 'Last month there was not a single day on which we had even one full measure of rice. If he had anything at all he would not have left the children without anything to fill their bellies. He's too good a father for that.'

Shaking his head with an air of disbelief, Muniswami said, 'Would anybody say without any reason at all that he took it? There must be a grain of truth in it.'

She swore that it was not so. What else was there for her to say?

Muniswami, taking on the role of a judge, said, 'Look, till today we gave you the means to get a couple of measures of rice daily. Why? Because we took him to be one of us. From now on that's not so. It's to tell you this that we have brought you here. Why have we come to this decision? Because if we help a thief we are committing a crime.'

So they abandoned the family. Once again Alamelu tried to explain the true state of things. Calling on Almighty God to be her witness, she told her story.

Vallinayagam's heart melted a little and he said, 'Pichandi has gone off with the stuff. Maybe she doesn't know anything about it.'

Muniswami disagreed: 'Get away with you! What do you know about it? She's as much a thief as he is. They've hidden it.'

Sobbing, Alamelu once again swore it was not so. 'In the name of my four children, no!'

'Go. Be off with you.'

Alamelu went away. The scavengers had decided unanimously that there was no need to help her any more. Pichandi had committed the theft. Alamelu had hidden away what he had stolen.

The whole thing had been a trick played by the overseer Keshava Pillai to frighten Pichandi; it was the chance Chudala-muttu was looking for to break off with Pichandi; for when those poor, senseless creatures, the scavengers, all banded together it produced a serious situation.

The police came to the scavenger colony to look for Pichandi. They searched his hut. They took Alamelu along to the station. That day not a single scavenger went home. They were all too scared.

The next day Alamelu came back, dragging her steps and too weak to walk. Her four children sat huddled around her. The previous day they had had nothing to eat. What was she to do?

Alamelu was in a state of collapse. She had been all skin and bone: now her body was bloated. The eldest child went into town to beg. The second child was taken ill.

The wife of a thief merits no compassion; nor do his children. All the scavengers believed that Pichandi was guilty of theft. In accordance with Muniswami's strict orders, no one gave any assistance. If one gives help to a thief's dependants it is a serious crime! So the days passed by.

The ailing Alamelu was counting the days as they passed. She consoled her children by saying, 'When five more days have gone by, Father will come.' After he got back everything would be straightened out. Father would bring them food to eat. He would buy rice and tapioca. So the children looked forward to his return.

On the fifteenth day after Pichandi went away Alamelu was able to leave her bed and sit up. If somehow that day would end and another one dawn! If he did not come what would she and the children do? It would be enough if he came and took her and the children together away with him.

At night Alamelu did not sleep a wink. She was listening attentively for the sound of her husband's footsteps. So the dawn broke. But Pichandi did not come.

'Mother, why hasn't Father come?' The children began to ask their questions.

The next day and the day after that he still did not come. So a whole week went by.

One day at noon the overseer turned up along with a scavenger and his family. Alamelu and the children had to vacate the house. Taking two cooking pots, three curry pots and a couple of old mats, Alamelu, her body still bloated and swollen, went off with the children. A new family had come to live there.

Parenthood

When Chudalamuttu came home he did not see Valli. This was unusual. When he got back from work he would normally find her on the verandah. Today all the doors were open. From beyond them could be heard the sound of vomiting. Anxiously Chudalamuttu went to where it was coming from.

It was Valli who was vomiting! She was bent double with the force of it. She was choking.

'What is it, Valli?'

Wretched though she looked, she said, 'It's nothing.'

'Should I go and fetch the doctor?'

'There's no need.' When she felt a little better she stood up. Chudalamuttu was less anxious.

'What's the matter with you?'

She answered with a smile. When you ask sick people what they are suffering from, do they smile?

For a few days Valli had been unwell. Chudalamuttu had been asking what the reason was. She replied that it was nothing. She had also been spitting more than usual. On one occasion he had asked why that was, too. She had not been eating properly. Now she was vomiting. What sort of vomiting was it?

'What's wrong with you, Valli? Tell me.'

'I told you. Nothing.'

'Then what about this vomiting?'

'Oh! That's quite normal.'

'Normal? What do you mean normal?'

Once again a smile!

That day after eating Chudalamuttu did not go out anywhere. In the evening, while he was loosening the soil round the roots of some bushes he had planted in the garden, she was behind the house retching. What a nuisance this was! She said she was not ill; yet she was vomiting forcefully. When he asked why, she laughed.

She told him. Chudalamuttu picked her up in his arms and jumped around. That had been the meaning of the smile. When a woman tells her husband that she is pregnant, even if it is her tenth pregnancy, she will be shy.

Chudalamuttu's plans were going to be realised.

At dusk they decorated with garlands of flowers the part of the house set aside for worship. Through it spread the aroma of sandalwood and the eight kinds of perfume. It rose as far as the top floor of the big house of the well-to-do family which lay to the south of theirs. That day the wicks of their small brass lamps had a special brightness. At the time of worship Valli's hands were together and her eyes closed in an attitude of prayer. She realised that there were things to pray for. Didn't the child she was expecting need a long life? Didn't it need good health? A good position in life? For those things they must pray. With real sincerity they praised God. Even after Chudalamuttu had finished Valli was still praying. He stood watching her. A mother has many things to pray for on behalf of her child.

That night neither of them slept. Yet they did not say anything either. While Chudalamuttu was meditating on his plans Valli was thinking that what she carried in her womb was a great and powerful thing. Lying inside her was a child who would become an important man. She was giving him the gift of life.

The next evening Chudalamuttu brought back a bottle of pills for his wife. He had bought them at a druggist's in Mullaikkal. She asked him what they were for.

'For you to take. The wives of well-off people take these pills when they are expecting. The doctor told me.'

'Why do they take them?'

'You'll give birth without pain. The child will be strong.'

After that he asked her what she wanted, a boy or a girl. What she wanted was a boy. That was Chudalamuttu's wish too. But if the child were a girl? Then they would bring up a girl!

'When it's inside you,' asked Chudalamuttu, 'can you tell whether it's a boy or a girl?'

'They say that women who've already had children can tell.'

Each day they had something new to talk about and to think

about. Every day Chudalamuttu came back with something new that he had learnt. One day it would be the food an expectant mother should eat; another day it would be her routine. All that he told her she put into effect.

During this time Chudalamuttu did not manage to put anything by. There was so much to pay out! But there was a consolation. It was with that child as the centre that all his dreams would be realised. All this expenditure was for the child. Yet such liberal spending was not acceptable to Valli. In an effort to explain to her, Chudalamuttu said, 'What sort of person do you think will come out of your belly?'

She thought a little and then replied, 'What sort of person? Why, a scavenger's son!'

Chudalamuttu was thunderstruck. Such a thought had never occurred to him. What a frightful truth it was – that the child would be a scavenger's son!

Chudalamuttu gave her a piece of advice: 'You must not think this way. Yesterday in the Mullaikkal Ashram the holy man said that you must only think of good things. If you do, the child will grow up to be something. If you think of him as a scavenger's son, he will become a scavenger.'

'Then what should I think he's going to be?'

What was the child going to be? A judge? A doctor? Or president of the municipality? Chudalamuttu simply could not make up his mind. He had not thought about it.

When alone in the house, Valli would think about her child's future. In five months' time that angel would show himself. Once he was born, she would not have to sit alone. As for the way he looked – it was enough that he should be like his father.

Valli washed some old pieces of cloth, put them together and made a cradle out of them. She bought something to boil the water in. So she got ready for the birth of the child.

Inside the house it had been crying for a long time. So much crying! What were they doing to it in there? The birth had just taken place. Should it be crying so much? Did it have the strength for that? Chudalamuttu called out, 'Stop making it cry.'

The reply to that was suppressed laughter from the women inside the room. Chudalamuttu felt he had said something stupid.

Slowly the child's crying subsided. Yet they still did not bring it out. Is it not the father who has the right to see him first? No, that's the mother's privilege. But in any case they could bring him out now and take him straight back.

Chudalamuttu looked in through a crack in the door. There was nothing to be seen. He suddenly thought it was not right for him to be peeping like that. Three or four times he was about to tell them to bring the child out.

Once again the child began to cry. Again Chudalamuttu was anxious. If it cried like that, wouldn't it stop breathing? Once more he called out, 'Don't make it cry.'

From inside came the reply: 'We're giving him a bath.' It was his wife's voice.

After a while the door opened and the midwife came out carrying the baby.

When his eyes fell on the curled up, shivering baby, Chudalamuttu felt as if all his dreams were coming true. His eyes and heart were enjoying a sight they had never before experienced. Where had this child come from? Its eyes were lively and bright.

The midwife said, 'Take the baby.'

Chudalamuttu's hands stayed by his side. An old woman, who had come out of the room, said, 'First give ten chakrams and then take the child.'

Chudalamuttu found ten chakrams and gave them. But he was afraid to take the child in his arms. He was a scavenger. How could he take that child with hands that had cleaned out latrines? Yet he had to take it. He stretched out his arms and took the child. Then he immediately gave it back.

Never before had Chudalamuttu felt such an aversion to being a scavenger. It almost seemed that the child had the same aversion! Did it have a sense of smell? Even though a scavenger bathed he still stank. Would something bad happen to the child just because he touched it? He must grow up without coming close to a scavenger. Yet when he put the child in someone else's arms Chudalamuttu wanted to take him back again.

The midwife and the rest of them had gone. Chudalamuttu went into the confinement room. Valli had the child by her side and was lying on her bed. She smiled. It was a new sort of smile. As Chudalamuttu watched the child comfortably sleeping there, she asked, 'Why do you stare at him?'

There was a peremptory tone in her voice. Like a culprit Chudalamuttu replied, 'Oh, nothing. He's sleeping.'

With a bit torn off a piece of old cloth, she covered his naval. The cord was sticking out as if it didn't belong there. Chudalamuttu had no wish to move away from where he stood.

'What did you say he should be?' Valli asked.

Almost every day Chudalamuttu had been wondering what his son should be. But he was no nearer to making a decision. He must think about it again.

The size of his responsibility frightened Chudalamuttu. Asking what he should become was not an empty, trivial question. The child's mother was asking what he had decided to make of the child; or, more precisely, the child was asking.

As he stood there looking at the mother and child, he felt that they were in a different world from before, that their interests were now one and the same. Whatever the child asked through her, he must be prepared to give.

That indeed was true. But it was not enough that he should give. Chudalamuttu now had no rights, only responsibilities. As for the child's mother – her orders must now be obeyed.

When he went to work the next day he heard a baby crying in the house of Kurup, the lawyer. The lawyer's daughter's pregnancy had reached the end of its term and she had given birth the previous day. Here the child was a girl.

The lawyer's wife asked Chudalamuttu: 'When did the birth take place yesterday?'

'In the afternoon.'

'In that case it was under the influence of Pushya.'

Chudalamuttu said nothing, for he did not understand, and the lady went on: 'Is there any "foot"?'

Any foot! He could make neither head nor tail of that either. The child had arms and legs. It suffered from no physical defect. The woman laughed and said, 'No, not that. When the moon enters Pushya there are some inauspicious times. If a child is born on one of those days all sorts of bad things can happen to the mother or the father. That's what's meant by asking if there is any "foot".'

Chudalamuttu felt as though something hot and smouldering had been dropped inside him. To whom was the bad thing going to happen? The lady advised him: 'Ask Varyar, the astrologer. By drawing up a horoscope one can know everything.'

As it happened, it was Chudalamuttu who did the job of scavenger at the astrologer's house. On that very day he made arrangements for his child's horoscope.

When he returned home it was with a heavy heart. His face was less happy than usual. His body, too, was weary. The fortress of his aspirations had suffered a great blow. Its walls had cracked and even broken. If the child's horoscope was unfavourable . . . He prayed that it should not be so. What else could he do?

A few people came that day to see the new baby. Valli's friends! Chudalamuttu, whose nerves were on edge, was annoyed when he heard about this. He asked his wife: 'What did they come for?'

What a meaningless question! The reply that Valli gave was, 'It's a custom.'

'Custom? There's no need for anybody to come here.'

'If that's the way it is, then you should go to all the houses about and say that nobody need come. Such nonsense!'

She was standing up to him. He sensed that through this opposition her strength and authority increased. What if he were to hurl in her face the thing he had learnt earlier that day? But how would a mother be able to bear that?

Chudalamuttu's anger turned in another direction: 'They'll all be picking up my child and pawing him.'

The expression on her face changed slightly as she asked, '*Your* child?'

The question was a strange one, and at the same time profoundly significant. Chudalamuttu did not grasp its import. He was at a loss. He said with feeling, 'Yes, *my* child. Am I not its father?'

Valli said forcefully, 'All that is so. You are its father. There's no mistake about that. But you must remember God when you speak. It is weak and helpless. What if it were to die?'

Chudalamuttu was shocked. 'What a thing to say!'

'How do you mean? Remember it's God's. Don't say things like that.'

Chudalamuttu did not pursue it any further. He again slid into a state of uncontrollable anxiety. Had she, too, heard about what the lawyer's wife had told him?

He had heard some people say that it was better not to have babies and children. It seemed to Chudalamuttu that there was something in this. It would be less troublesome to be childless.

Chudalamuttu prayed that the child should have a long life. Even that was not enough. Should not the child's mother live too? So in the second place he prayed that she should live long. Were even these two things adequate? Should not he live too? In this way he prayed for many, many things, a hundred or more. Even then there were more things left to pray for.

He did not see any such anxieties in Valli. Why was it so? Did she not love the child as much as he did? Should she not pray for him to live a long time, as he had prayed for her to do? Was it not necessary for the child that he, the father, should have a long life?

They were very careful in bringing up the child; they wrapped him in flannel, powdered him and so on. He grew up like the child of a prince. His mother? Was she not the one who must bring him up? Valli's position and status increased. Every day Chudalamuttu would bring back fine things that he had bought. She must eat. She must be in the best of health. Was it not the milk from her breasts that the child drank? Because it was she who was taking care of him in everything, she must be scrupulously clean. Every single day he made some change in their mode of life.

When Chudalamuttu went into the houses with his bucket and shovel he was looking at and studying things to do with children; ways of bringing up children. Now he even knew a few medicines for the treatment of children.

His child must be given a name. He knew the names of all the children in Mullaikkal Ward; he had made it his business to know. What name should they choose? As well as a name, his son needed a pet-name.

Chudalamuttu named his son Mohanan. The pet-name was to be Baby. Valli was in agreement. Chudalamuttu gave strict instructions that from that day onwards the child should be called nothing but Baby.

When she knew that the scavenger's son was called Mohanan the wife of the lawyer Kurup burst out laughing. This laughter did not just make Chudalamuttu feel small; it shocked and petrified him. It was not only the mockery that filled the laughter; it also sounded as if a scavenger had no right to give his child a name.

When he left that house, burning questions were tormenting Chudalamuttu. Did they not accept his son as a member of the human race? Could he not give him the name he chose? There was no need for others to love him; but did not he himself have the right to do so?

Furious, Chudalamuttu let out a roar. He was deciding all over again that his name should be Mohanan and that he should have Baby as a pet-name. He wanted to let them know that the scavenger's son had a pet-name.

He went to the doctor's house and called out to the doctor like someone who was out of his mind: 'Yesterday was the day my child received a name.' Chudalamuttu thought the doctor would ask what the name was, but this was not a matter of interest to anyone. Chudalamuttu said without being asked, 'His name is Mohanan.'

Chudalamuttu then watched carefully to see if there was any change of expression on the doctor's face. With a burning desire to be avenged on the world, he waited to see what effect it would have.

It seemed as if the doctor's lips moved a little. Eventually he said that he had treated a Sukeshini who was losing her hair and a Sulochana who had trouble with her eyes, notwithstanding the fact that their names were supposed to mean 'lovely hair' and 'beautiful eyes'. By the same token, was it to be supposed that Mohanan would necessarily be 'charming'?

Chudalamuttu went to the Reddiar's house and said that his son's name was Mohanan and that the child had a pet-name. In the same way he went and told them in all the houses. It was an attack on their superior attitudes. A scavenger had called his son Mohanan. Chudalamuttu now thought of this as a challenge. From now on he would challenge them in many ways. But he had no idea what the nature of these challenges would be.

The wife of the municipal president asked, 'So is he going to be called Baby, the scavenger?' Then she, too, laughed.

The words 'He's not a scavenger' were on the tip of Chudalamuttu's tongue. But he suppressed them. Let them learn that later.

Chudalamuttu returned home that day more pensive than on any previous occasion. The thought of vengeance was a strong fire that was consuming his heart. He would make them call the child 'Baby' . . . But it was a pity that he had been born a scavenger's son.

His child was lying face downwards on the verandah and playing. Valli was in the kitchen. When he went up to the child, he saw that it had dirtied itself and was burying its small hand in the mess and playing with it.

'Hey! Valli!' Chudalamuttu was beside himself with anger. 'Hey!'

Hearing him shout in an unusual way, she came out. She saw her husband standing there really angry. She had no idea why. Pointing to the child, Chudalamuttu asked, 'What on earth's this?'

Valli picked up the child. Chudalamuttu got angrier still. She thought nothing of it, that the child should be lying there like that. He began to scold her. Valli retorted, 'Children are like this sometimes.'

'My child mustn't be like this.'

'Then what do you think you have been doing all day?' asked Valli. 'The child belongs to someone with that sort of job.'

'So must he be like that too?'

Valli did not bother to reply. She thought there was nothing much behind his outburst.

When the child made the sound 'mma' Valli would call out, 'What is it, my son?' She had the right to say that. But when the child made the sound 'ppa' Chudalamuttu was afraid to answer. He was a scavenger. And the child? What was the child? Valli was annoyed: 'Oh, so that's how it is. When the child calls, you don't say a word in reply.'

It was not because Chudalamuttu did not wish to reply. It was not that he did not wish to establish a claim to his position as the child's father. Chudalamuttu wanted to claim the child as his. But he was afraid! The child must not know that his father was a scavenger; he must not be told. The child must not get a sense of inferiority in that way.

Valli did not understand. What she said was, 'However important he grows up to be, his father is still his father.'

And she then asked the child: 'Isn't that so, my son?'

Making a happy sound, the child jumped towards him. Chudalamuttu did not pick him up. Instead he said, 'Why should he know? I'll bring him up. I'll make him into something. That'll be enough. Why should he know all that?'

'Then isn't he ever to know?' she asked. 'What sort of crazy talk is this?'

Having thought for a short while, Chudalamuttu went on: 'He needn't know he's a scavenger's son.'

'Why shouldn't he know?'

'It'll bring him down in the world.'

'It'll do nothing of the sort. If he'd been a fatherless child it would be a different matter. And who's he to say is his father?'

That, too, was a problem. Who would he say was his father?

One by one Chudalamuttu listed all the difficulties he would face if he were the son of a scavenger. No matter how important a person he became, a scavenger's son would suffer some loss of status.

'He needn't have been born our son. Isn't that so?'

'What is it you're trying to say? I don't know.'

'Just that. He needn't have been born.'

Chudalamuttu described the things that had happened after the child had been named Mohanan. If he said anything about his son to the other scavengers they, too, laughed. A scavenger could not have a nice child. He could not give him a good name. Such a child should not have a pet-name. A scavenger should not be affectionate towards his child. Then could not a child who was born to become somebody of importance be born the son of a scavenger? Was not his very birth a denial of his freedom?

No matter how much he said, Valli did not understand his reasoning. Unlike Chudalamuttu she did not live in an imaginary world. Her only wish was that her child should be better off than them. When she said he must be better off, she did not build castles in the air, speculating on what he should be. Beyond the feeling that he should be better off, she had no thoughts on the subject of his destiny. Her constant prayer was that he should live a long time. That was her greatest desire. She was his mother.

Chudalamuttu used to spend hours just watching the child. The day it smiled for the first time was an important one in his life. When he saw it fall on its face Chudalamuttu would get scared and cry out. The child would bang its nose on the ground. On the day it began to crawl Chudalamuttu became more anxious. Would the child's knees not get rubbed raw?

There was great pleasure in seeing the child grow up. But in that happiness there also was a sadness; a feeling of desolation. The fatherly affection which he could not show, which he suppressed, broke the walls of the poor fellow's heart. When the child rolled over on its stomach he could not touch it but would just stand there. Chudalamuttu had decided not to touch him. A self-imposed curse! He would be satisfied if he could call him 'son' on the odd occasion. But he had decided not to do even this. If he did this sort of thing, there would be impediments in Mohanan's life. He would withdraw; he would ask nothing of life. Just let the boy grow up!

As he witnessed the child growing up, Chudalamuttu felt satisfaction. Yet here was a father who completely denied himself the right to touch his son, to call his son 'son'. This was the result of entertaining unrealistic desires; this was the result of feeling that he was unclean.

Mohanan had a golden thread about his waist. He had a bangle. Chudalamuttu compared his own child with every child he met. His child was handsome and gifted. He felt he must show everyone his child – and he must surprise them.

One evening the parents dressed the child nicely and went to the beach. Valli, carrying the child, walked in front; Chudalamuttu followed behind. It was a beautiful summer evening. Many people had come to the beach to take the air. The big people of the town! Their fine children were running, jumping and rolling about on the white sand. Chudalamuttu was looking to see if any of those big people noticed his own child.

When he saw the children lying and playing on the sand, Mohanan, too, wanted to get down. He pulled away from his mother's hip. A couple, a little distance away, noticed his obstinacy. The woman said to her husband, 'Look there, at that bright child, he's giving his mother some trouble.'

The husband said, 'It doesn't look like her child.'

'That's true. Such a lively child.'

Taking a careful look the husband said, 'She's a road-sweeper. It's not her child.'

Chudalamuttu heard the whole conversation. His son was a lively child! Did he not have the right to feel proud?

For a mother it is not enough that a child calls her 'Mother'. Even if there is no father, she will teach the child to say 'Father'. Even if she does not teach it to do so, the child will come to say 'Father' of its own accord. Even if the father forbids it, still it will say it. In a house where the father loves the child more than his own life, in a house where there is no weakening of the husband–wife relationship, will a child not call for the father? Will the mother fail to point to the father?

Mohanan would call his father, laugh when he saw his father, stand at the gate waiting for his father – all these things. Nobody can prevent all this. But Chudalamuttu had been standing aloof. He had not picked up the child; he had not kissed him. Mohanan had not learnt the pleasure of those things.

See what a sacrifice that is – to deny the pleasure that all living things long for!

A certain desire grew up in Mohanan. No one could say where it came from. Perhaps it is something a child is born with. To suppress it would be an impossibility.

Lying on his back on his mother's lap he said, 'Mum! Today I'm going to eat with Father.'

This is the sort of thing that thrills a mother when she hears it from her child. She agreed. Then came a dangerous question: 'Why doesn't Father pick me up?' What answer could Valli give? He went on: 'I'm going to ask Father to pick me up.' He went further: 'Today I'll only give Father a kiss. I won't give you one.'

At midday Valli called him many times to come and eat. He refused to eat. He was waiting for his father to arrive.

Valli doubted whether his desires were going to be realised. She decided she must talk to her husband and tell him to give up this mad obstinacy. All the things the boy wanted – did he not have a right to them? Were they not things he was bound to want? He had begun to ask questions. He could no longer be denied.

Mohanan saw his father in the distance when he came back worn-out from his day's toil. He ran indoors. 'Mother! Put my plate along with Father's when you serve the rice!'

'You must tell him that yourself. If I tell him, he won't listen.'

Mohanan pulled a long face. 'I won't. You must tell him.' He rubbed his eyes and started to cry.

When Chudalamuttu arrived he saw his son standing there like that. Curious, he asked, 'What's the child crying for?'

Valli replied with a smile: 'He wants to sit down beside you.'

Chudalamuttu was taken aback. Yes, he was really taken aback. He had never imagined that such a demand would be made. The boy wants to eat rice that has been mixed with the curry by his father's hands, the same hands that have cleaned out the latrines. How can he allow this? Yet how can he deny it? From now on his son is going to call him Father openly.

Mohanan was standing inside crying. Chudalamuttu once again experienced the stench of the latrines where he worked. For years that stench had been stuck in his nose. He thought of all the latrines he was familiar with. Daily with spade and shovel he scooped up that filth into the bucket and emptied it into the cart – and all the time it would splash and fall on his body . . . and he was a human being! A man with a heart, mind and five senses! Why did he have the capacity to produce offspring? Was it in order that there should be more scavengers? Would it be possible for his son to become somebody of note? No! It seemed to Chudalamuttu that he should take a pot with him in the morning. Everything he got from the houses, the previous day's mouldy *payasam*, or the water the rice had been washed in, or the stale porridge – all this he should put in the pot, set it on the muck cart and bring it back to give to the child. That was the way he should grow up. A scavenger's child could not grow up without eating that dirt. Even if he did not give it to the child, the child would want it. That dirt was something a scavenger's child found tastier than biscuits, for a relish for that sort of thing was inherited.

Yet Chudalamuttu fought against these thoughts. The child

must grow up without knowing he was a scavenger's son, without eating that dirt. The stench of a latrine must make him vomit. He must feel disgust at the sight of a scavenger. He must hold his nose when he goes near his father. He must not address his father as 'Father'.

Within those few minutes Chudalamuttu made up his mind on something: in his role as father he only wished for one or two things in future years. When he became old he would like to be able to stay quietly in one room; to get something to eat three times a day. The earthen pot that symbolised his job as a scavenger should be irrecoverably buried in the night-soil depot. No matter how important a person his son became, it was enough for Chudalamuttu if he should get those few things. Just those! And he was ready to renounce even those. He could do without them too; he wanted nothing. It was enough if Mohanan, like other people, simply addressed him as 'scavenger'; let him use that form of address.

How sad it all was! A scavenger, having established a family and brought up a son, was going to make him into somebody of note. Chudalamuttu understood how impossible that was. As soon as such a child is born, the wives of scavengers will kiss him. He has no right to a good name. Even if that child gets excrement on his hands and eats it, his mother will not care. He will feel no disgust for his father who spends his time scooping up filth.

Nevertheless Chudalamuttu determined to make some sort of effort. That day Chudalamuttu did not eat.

Childhood

Mohanan had no friends. The next-door neighbours were well-to-do. Beyond them were the houses of poor people. All around there were children. But the scavenger's son had never been to play with any of them.

Further away still, at the home of the millionaire businessman, could be heard the hubbub of children fixing a net and playing a ball game. Fascinated, Mohanan stood watching the yellow ball flying to and fro over the net which could be seen over the wall. The rich man's child, like a Japanese doll on the verandah of the mansion, and Mohanan in his house stood looking at each other; they were making signs. But between them was a high stone wall.

Mohanan also watched orphaned and homeless children in the street in front of the house shouting and howling and generally kicking up a shindy as they played. One boy ran ahead; another chased after him. How far would they dash like that? What fun it must be! . . . Getting interested in their games, Mohanan would laugh and shout along with them. In the rainy season they would sail paper boats along the drains and skip after them. At noon on a sunny day they would jump in the stream on the far side of the road and splash about in the water. And for so long, too! He was struck dumb by the freedom enjoyed by these beggar children.

Some of the children asked him to join them. Others pulled faces at him. And there were some who frightened him by clenching their fists as if to punch him. Yet he was very eager to go beyond the fence and play with them.

One day when Mohanan was standing at the gate a small boy came up to him. Mohanan was chewing a piece of bread. The boy asked if he would give him a little bit and Mohanan did so.

The boy started talking: 'Will you come and play?'

'My mother will be cross.'

Thus he became immersed in an enjoyable conversation. He talked of so many things! When the rest of the boys organised another kind of game, the boy got up and went off in the middle of the conversation. Mohanan's mother called to say it was time for his bath.

So Mohanan acquired a friend. He would tell Mohanan of all the things that happened downtown: the story of the dog that died after being run over by a car; the story of the man in the coffee shop who poured hot water over a boy; the story of the policeman who chased after the four of them. In this way Mohanan heard lots of interesting stories. What fun it would be to go wherever one wanted in the town and see all that went on!

Unknown to his mother, Mohanan would take bread and bananas and give them to his friend. Somehow he had a feeling that his mother should know nothing about it. And Valli did not know of it.

One day Mohanan waited a long time for his friend. That day none of the boys were to be seen there, and Mohanan felt very dejected. The next day, too, he did not see his friend. On the third day he turned up at noon.

There had a been a wedding at a rich man's house in town. For two days there had been a big feast, and he had been there. Not only he, but crowds of other boys had been there too.

'We ate and ate till we were sick. It was so nice. We had no end of things to eat.'

Then he beat on his bulging belly like a drum.

Mohanan stood looking at the beggar boy in amazement. It seemed he had to go right away. There was a temple festival in Mullaikkal. There would be a procession with five elephants; and there would be fireworks. He was planning to go there and he asked Mohanan, 'Are you coming?'

'I can't come. My mother won't let me.'

'Then I'll be off.'

'Will your mother back home agree?' asked Mohanan.

'I don't have a mother,' said the boy casually. 'I've no home either. Well, I'll be going. It's time for the festival.'

Shouting out a snatch of some song, he shot off. For a long time Mohanan stood watching him. He was able to see so many things!

So the friendship grew stronger every day. His mother found out about it and forbade him to have anything to do with children of that sort. Yet the friendship was not something that could be prevented. When his mother was not looking, Mohanan would go to the gate and stand there looking at the boy; they would talk together. The beggar boy, as far as Mohanan was concerned, was a source of wonderment. He had no father, no mother, no home. So he went around freely.

Mohanan found out a number of things from the beggar boy. Every day he and his companions would see Mohanan's father in Mullaikkal. Mohanan's father was a scavenger.

So Mohanan finally got an answer to his question. He used to ask his mother where it was that his father went every day. She would reply that he went to work. When the boy, in an attempt to satisfy his curiosity, asked what work, she would say that he went to a job that would provide the means to buy biscuits, bananas, rice and so on. Now he had found out that his father went to Mullaikkal and that he was a 'scavenger'.

The beggar boy, too, had had a father; he, too, had been a scavenger. That scavenger's name had been Pichandi. He knew his father's name, but not his own name.

Mohanan had yet another question to ask his mother: 'Mother, what does the word "scavenger" mean?'

Too put out to give an answer, Valli got angry with him. 'Why do you ask such pointless things?'

She threatened to beat him. Mohanan got scared.

That evening Valli told Chudalamuttu all about it, how Mohanan had asked what scavenger meant!

Chudalamuttu was shocked. It was yet another blow to his castles in the air. But, contrary to Valli's expectations, there was no storm of rage. After a little while he said with a sigh, 'I knew it wouldn't be possible to keep it from him. But he needn't have known so soon.' After some time Chudalamuttu, full of despair, said, 'You were right, Valli! It won't be possible for our son to get such a good position in life. That's what I think about all the time.'

The cold despair in her husband's words touched Valli's heart. She, too, understood that sad reality. Although, being suspicious of them, she had opposed her husband's vain expectations, she had still cherished the thought that her son would one day become somebody. While sitting alone she had thought about his becoming somebody important, about its possibilities. She could see thousands upon thousands of obstacles.

So husband and wife together arrived at the same point. Chudalamuttu began to speak further: 'This is what I'm always thinking of. Some day or other he'll find out he's a scavenger's son. Wherever he goes, he's a scavenger's son. These are two things to be afraid of.'

Valli too had something to say: 'I think of it as well! Is there any sense in him pretending he's not a scavenger's son? Just think a bit: where will he find a woman to marry him? Will he get anyone other than a scavenger's daughter?'

'No. That's true. But I won't bring him up as a scavenger's son. That's definite. Though he is a scavenger's son, his son shouldn't be one.'

Valli said with a sigh, 'That child will be the son of a scavenger's son.'

Thinking for a while, Chudalamuttu said, 'Yes.'

'Who was it who first made scavengers?' asked Valli.

'Do you think of such things too?'

'I do. Once in a while I think of them. I never used to think of such things. Now I've started thinking on those lines.'

'Do you dislike being a scavenger?'

'How am I to answer such a question? Is it possible for me to dislike it?'

He took this to mean that his wife thought like him.

To clear up a doubt she had, Valli asked, 'Will there be a time when there are no scavengers?'

'Oh, I don't know!'

'There can't be such a time. Ever. How can there? If there are latrines, must there not be scavengers?'

What Chudalamuttu was thinking about was not the doubt in Valli's mind. He couldn't care less whether there would always be scavengers or not. He himself would have to live as a scavenger. Mohanan knew his father was a scavenger. He would know its degradation too; in future years he would have to face obstacles. Would his son have the strength to overcome those obstacles?

'Supposing we don't want this work?' asked Valli.

Chudalamuttu replied, 'Have the house and compound materialised yet? What the president said was that we must let him have five hundred rupees more for that. If we manage it, I'll chuck this job. These days it's not as easy to save as before.'

The problem that always frightened Valli made her even more worried: what had they given in all? Was there a receipt for it? Would the president cheat them? If he did, what could be done about it?

Chudalamuttu convinced her as to the precise amount. The president was not a man to operate that sort of a swindle. He would buy the house and garden for him.

'May God Almighty protect us,' was all that Valli had to say in reply.

They began to educate lawyer Kurup's daughter's child at home. He – Mohanan – must be admitted to a school. That was a new problem.

Near where they lived a man ran a sort of kindergarten for a few children. Chudalamuttu decided that if he put him there to study for a short while he would be able to get him admitted to a school. So one afternoon he went there.

The teacher was an orthodox man of the sort who smears sacred ashes on his forehead, sandalwood paste on his body and so on, and wears a topknot. Chudalamuttu said why he had come and the teacher asked, 'Aren't you the scavenger who lives next to the wealthy landowner?'

'Yes.'

In a rather serious tone of voice the teacher asked, 'What made you think of bringing your boy here to study?'

'It's nearby.'

'Hm! Anyway, it's not possible here.' Keeping his eyes on Chudalamuttu's face, the teacher continued, 'It's not possible here. You understand? How on earth could you be so presumptuous? You thought you could bring your children here and have them sit next to these children, didn't you? That's a good one.'

Chudalamuttu saw all the children who were sitting in the teacher's room. Many of them were known to him: one was the child of a woman who ran a small restaurant on the other side of the *coir* factory; another was a rickshaw-puller's son; yet another was from a family of traders. His child was more alert than any child there. Chudalamuttu was about to say so on the spot. The next moment he thought, what was the point of saying it?

Chudalamuttu's next attempt was at a government school a little way off. He went and saw the headmaster at his home and was told that he would be given an answer the next day. When he went the next day the headmaster said that according to the regulations he had more children in the class than he should have and that as a result it was not possible. He would need the permission of the assistant inspector to get into another school. When he went elsewhere, it was some other excuse.

He was well aware of the reason why his son could not gain admission to a school. It was because the child was a scavenger's son, and because of that alone!

One day Chudalamuttu got Mohanan ready in shorts and shirt and took him along with him. He thought he would let them see the boy. The headmaster liked him; good, a fine boy. He seemed like a boy from a good family. But this one, too, found an excuse.

It had never been known for a scavenger to get his child admitted to school. It had never happened that a scavenger's child had been sent to school. How could that unwritten law be broken?

It was essential that his son should be taught to read and write; only if the boy could read and write would he be satisfied. What if he gave the headmaster a bribe? Chudalamuttu thought it might then be possible. He approached the overseer, who said that if he gave him twenty rupees he would undertake to see that it was arranged.

If it's twenty, then it's twenty. Chudalamuttu agreed. It was the most vital thing in Chudalamuttu's life. One day a week later the overseer informed him that the headmaster had agreed to admit the boy. But there were two conditions. Someone else should be designated as the boy's guardian. Then, as regards fees, he would have to give the headmaster at least two rupees a month.

Chudalamuttu agreed to that too. So a child called Mohanan joined the first class of the Grant School as the nephew of the municipal president's driver.

That day was a red-letter day for Chudalamuttu and Valli. As

for the half-starved headmaster in the school, his monthly income
went up to ten rupees.

There was no other child in the school who went there looking
so neat and clean. No one would have guessed that he was a
scavenger's son; they were very particular about not letting
anyone think he was. As they were trying so hard, and as the boy's
education was more important than anything else in his parents'
life, Valli's mind was still dwelling on their problems. How far
would they be able to educate him? Until that day no one among
the Alleppey scavengers had ever sent his son to be educated.
Mohanan had had the luck to enter school after the payment of a
twenty-rupee bribe. But would it be possible for this to continue?

When the excitement of making the firm decision to get his son
admitted to school and the happiness of getting the decision put
into effect had subsided the father began to think further about the
situation. Would it be possible for his son's education to continue?
What would the obstacles be in the future? For how long would it
be possible to educate him? How would he end up?

Once again wife and husband were in agreement. They had
reached a point where their opinions coincided. When Valli said
again that their lofty aspirations were not going to be realised,
Chudalamuttu agreed with her. He also mentioned something else
that had occurred to him: 'Do you know why our kid was not
admitted to school? If a scavenger's children start getting educated — then people worry that there will no longer be any
scavengers.'

Chudalamuttu elaborated further: 'If we know how to write
then we won't want to be scavengers.'

Valli agreed that that was so. Who were those schools that one
saw all over the country actually for? 'One thing's for certain,' she
said, 'they won't let scavengers and beggars study.'

Meanwhile the beggar boy used to stand in the road every
morning waiting for Mohanan. He would go with him as far as the
school. Each day Valli would give her son a chakram to spend.
With it he would buy peanuts and candies and other things to eat.
When school was over the beggar boy, who had been loitering
around all day eating whatever he could get hold of, would come
back again with his belly blown up like a balloon! He would go
along with Mohanan as far as his house.

So, unbeknown to Chudalamuttu and Valli, their friendship developed.

When he returned home from school Mohanan had many things to tell his mother. His teacher's *dhoti* is torn open; he gets very angry with all the children. He asks each one what they have had to eat. One day a boy asked the teacher, 'Sir, what did you have this morning?'

He had had nothing to eat.

Mohanan asked his mother, 'Why didn't teacher eat anything, Mother?'

In his class there were several children who did not go and have a meal at midday. There was nothing in the house. There were some who came in the morning without taking even *kanji* or coffee. Some had skin trouble; some came dressed in tattered old clothes. As he was telling his story he suddenly remembered something important: 'Mother, that Raman Nair who sits next to me stinks! Gosh, how he stinks!' As if he could smell it all over again, Mohanan covered his nose with his hand and said, 'Tomorrow I'll ask teacher to let me sit somewhere else.'

After hearing all this his mother said, 'Fine. And what did my boy learn today?'

'Oh! We learnt one or two letters. We learnt to count up to ten. The teacher doesn't teach anything. He's so tired. His main job is drinking cold water.'

He wrote down the letters he had learnt to show her.

Some time after this Mohanan persistently plagued Valli in the morning. He didn't want the shorts and shirt he had worn the previous day; he had not been using enough talcum powder; he must use a nice sweet-smelling soap for his bath. Until that day he had never been so insistent. Angrily Valli asked, 'What's wrong with the shorts you wore yesterday? They're still clean.'

Rubbing his eyes he answered, 'All the children say I stink and run away from me holding their noses.'

Suddenly Valli knew what it was all about. A scavenger stinks; so a scavenger's son stinks too. It was a spiteful trick played by those nasty children. It was the enmity born of the teacher's insistence on an earlier occasion that they should all come to class looking as clean as Mohanan!

She gave way to her son's obduracy. But even so the children would not stop running away and holding their noses. The mother bathed and dressed him, and with tears in her eyes she kissed him, saying, 'My poor, unfortunate son.' Throughout his life that smell would stay with him. Even beyond that, would it not still be there!

With pain in her heart, Valli told her husband about this. What a wretched state of affairs! Chudalamuttu, too, felt pain in his heart. He said they would have many more griefs and sorrows like this to bear. Unhesitatingly Valli replied, 'It's no good. You will have to find a different job.'

'What about the house and compound?'

'You must get some other job and make money to buy it with.'

'That's true.'

'Then we must leave this place. My child must not suffer any more insults like this. He has found out he's a scavenger's son; but at least when he grows up let him not suffer this disgrace.'

Chudalamuttu agreed with that too. But there was another difficulty – the money they had entrusted to the president! He had said that he would provide a fair part of what was needed to buy the house and compound. Believing that promise, Chudalamuttu had worked faithfully. Without working too much longer he might get that amount.

Valli's resolve was that he should stop work straight away, and she stood firm on that. 'If he's not inclined to give us the extra, we don't want it. We must get back the money we have handed over to him.'

Chudalamuttu said nothing. He was thinking about all this. Valli's hatred of being a scavenger was even greater than his.

In the sleepless night that followed, Chudalamuttu examined his whole life. It was the first time he had looked back in this way. His father had been love itself. He had lived only for his son. When he thought of Ishukkumuttu's death and the events which followed it, Chudalamuttu's eyes filled with tears. The decomposed and disfigured corpse, the sight of the dogs at the foot of the mango tree digging it up, the fact that there was only one person to stand by him – Pichandi! Dear old Pichandi! How often he had provided him with food, with no thought of any return!

Pichandi's only concern had been to praise Chudalamuttu wherever he went . . . Was old Pichandi still alive today? Were the children? To have destroyed that family – Chudalamuttu's heart burnt like fire. All his nerves were taut. His mouth was parched . . . Chudalamuttu thought he could see Sundiran, whom he had known from the time he was small, standing before him with tears streaming from his eyes . . . Then he could hear a pitiful cry: 'Mother!'

When they took the mother to hospital her children were crying. Then he heard another shout and the response it called forth: 'Ammu!'

'Husband!'

Chudalamuttu closed his eyes. He put his hands over his ears. But this is not something one can close one's eyes to, or block one's ears to. If you do these things, the scenes become even clearer; the sounds can be heard in more detail . . . The memories would remain to remind him that orphaned families had been shattered, ties of friendship broken.

Chudalamuttu wondered how he could have acted in this way. He could not believe any of the things he had done. How had he had the nerve to do all this? . . . Which of the devils had possessed him? He recalled the first time his wife had opposed him. It was that day – the day when they mercilessly took Sundiran's wife from all that was dear to her and sent her to die. On all occasions when he had traded humanity and common sense for money, she had opposed him; he had considered her to be a person with many faults. But all she said was true . . . The son of a scavenger! The son of a scavenger! What she had said was true. He would always be a scavenger's son, no matter what.

Chudalamuttu struck a match and lit the lamp. Mohanan was curled up asleep. A scavenger's son! The name Mohanan did not suit him. The laughter of the lawyer Kurup's wife was justified.

Chudalamuttu cursed the day when Ishukkumuttu had fallen ill. It was then that he had accepted a scavenger's job as a means of livelihood and gone out carrying the bucket and shovel. If he had not done so, this child who was lying asleep would not have become a scavenger's son. What weakness and folly that had been! Chudalamuttu did not remember wanting the work of scavenger

when he was younger . . . It had been another mistake to suppose
he could go up in the world while staying in that job.

Now what? Give up all that he had achieved so far? What other
job could he do?! Would the president release him? He was a
weapon in the hands of the municipality to destroy his friends. His
friends . . . Yes, what were they if not his friends? As Valli had
said, who are they if not his own people? Is not he, too, a
scavenger? Like the child of any other scavenger, is not the one
sleeping here a scavenger's son? To pretend that he was superior
to the others – Chudalamuttu felt that he had deceived him.

Yet he would still try to get ahead. When he had money his son
would not be a scavenger's son. Just wait, just wait and see
whether his son could not get anyone but a scavenger's daughter.

One day the youngster came home crying. The teacher, who had a
very bad temper, had beaten him in school. He didn't want to go to
his class any more.

When his mother took off his shorts and looked she could see
three marks on his thigh where he had been hit. It was too much
for her and she asked anxiously. 'My dear son, why did he beat
you?'

'He said, "Aren't you a scavenger's son? If I tell you, you won't
understand," and he beat me. If that schoolmaster tells us
anything, we can't understand.'

Is that the way it is? Is it the case that if you teach a scavenger's
son he won't learn? It seemed to Valli that her son was very bright.
She had also gathered that he was a good pupil. Even though she
had never learnt to read he told her everything he had learnt. At
home he recited what he had studied at school. Maybe he could
have learnt even more. And then to claim that he won't understand! If a scavenger's son goes to school one must also listen to
that; and on top of it he must take beatings.

Mohanan had another complaint: 'Mother, please tell Dad not
to be a scavenger! That must be why he doesn't let me eat with
him. Tomorrow he'd better not go.'

Little though he knows about such matters, the boy is beginning
to say this sort of thing. Not just saying, either; he is ordering. For,
to Valli, it sounded like an order. 'Please tell Dad not to be a

scavenger.' Does he know why he is a scavenger? He must know. If not, would he speak with such assurance? Whatever the truth might be, she was afraid to throw any further light on the matter.

He asked her again: 'Will you tell Dad, Mother?'

Valli agreed to tell him. Mohanan was thrilled. Not only was he going to sit down with his father to eat, he would no longer be the target of ridicule at the school. He was chattering on about it, when he stopped to ask, 'What is a scavenger's job, Mother?'

A tricky question! He did not know what a scavenger's job was. Valli was lost for words. 'If I tell you, you won't understand.'

'You're just like the schoolmaster.'

The next moment she wondered whether it would not be better to let him know the truth. Why hide it? He would find out eventually. Was it not better that he should get to know about it when he was at home? Yet Valli was afraid to come out with it. Holding her son close to her, she kissed the top of his head and said, 'Son, we are poor people! Just poor people!'

'Then does the word scavenger mean poor people, Mother?'

'Yes.'

Mohanan's curiosity was not entirely satisfied. Yet he did not get an answer. But the next day, when the boys in his class made fun of him by calling him a scavenger's son, he would at least have some answer to give them. He felt relieved.

The scavenger's son did not know what the word 'scavenger' meant. But other children of his age knew. They knew because they felt an aversion to scavengers.

Valli told her husband of their son's demand and said, 'There's no way round it. You will have to get a different job. You must get one before he finds out everything.'

Chudalamuttu did not have a satisfactory answer to give her. He had seen the municipal president and mentioned the matter of the house and compound. The president had again said that he would buy it for him. Chudalamuttu had explained that it would do if he got back the money he had given him for safe-keeping. Then the president had lost his temper.

Valli asked very anxiously, 'Then it may be that we shan't get the money?'

'It's not like that! It's not that he won't give it.'

'If that's so, couldn't he just let you have it?'

'It's not the way you think; it's because I was in a hurry that he got angry.'

Valli did not believe any of this. Inside her a voice kept saying that they would not get the money back. Yet she was afraid even to say that they would not get it. She asked, 'Supposing you don't get the money, what happens if you decide not to keep this job?'

'If I pack in the job, won't it make it a bit difficult?'

Valli's acute mind made her ask again, 'Then we won't get it?'

Slightly annoyed, Chudalamuttu said, 'Who says that's what it means?'

Chudalamuttu found a way of changing his job. They were thinking of appointing a watchman for a burial ground in the municipality. There was a chance that he might get the job. In Valli's view even that would be good enough.

The following day Mohanan came home to accuse his mother of telling him a lie. When his mother asked him what he meant by that, he said, 'Didn't you tell me yesterday that a scavenger is a poor person? A scavenger is not a poor person.'

He had found out!

Mohanan continued, 'When I was walking along at midday today there was a man pulling a cart. I ran with my hand over my nose. Then a boy told me that was a scavenger. Mother! Does Dad go along pulling a cart like that?'

Valli had expected that a very tricky situation would arise when Mohanan found out what the word 'scavenger' meant. Yet he was asking in the way he normally spoke. Knowing what it meant did not seem to have made all that much difference. Even if he had found it out directly, there would have been no difficulty. Maybe when he knew what was in the cart – even then he would not get perturbed. Slowly, without any emotion, Valli answered his question: 'Yes. Dad, too, goes along pulling a cart like that.'

The boy's mind worked in a different way from the one they had anticipated: 'Poor Dad will sweat in the sun too.'

Cholera

In Kottuval, on the edge of the road near Chavadi Bridge, the morning light showed a dead beggar lying cold and stiff in front of a tea-shop. He had passed motion and vomited. The abandoned body was covered with all the flies in town.

It was a bit of a nuisance for the owner of the tea-shop. Suppose he decided to move it away from there . . . The man in the neighbouring shop, who made a living selling tobacco and betel leaves, advised him not to do it.

'You'll find yourself facing a murder charge. Better not touch it!'

'Then what's to be done? What a pest! Couldn't he die somewhere else?'

'You should go and tell them at the municipal offices or the police station.'

That would raise another difficulty. If you go and say something at that sort of place it involves some expenditure. The lawyer's clerk who lived nearby explained how he saw it: 'If you contact the police they'll finish you off. As for the municipality, do you know what a crafty bloke that overseer is? It seems to me you should let it lie there. They'll hear about it and come and take it away.'

Everybody around thought this was sound advice. The rickshaw puller Nanu also gave the lawyer's clerk a testimonial: 'You see how everything is straightened out when people who know their way around come along?'

Business in the shop went on as usual. The tea-shop owner realised that, because of the abandoned corpse lying there, what he made that day was a little more than usual. Towards evening he had run out of snacks. Usually at that time there were some left over on the shelf where he kept them. The people who came to look at the dead body stood there for a little while, went inside and had something to drink and a bite to eat, and then went off. Fine; the tea-shop owner congratulated himself on doing so well out of it.

In the evening the lawyer's clerk Tanu Pillai had another piece of advice: 'At night-time, Mummu, you'll have to watch out in case some dog comes and bites and tears at it. It'll complicate things if they see marks on the body.'

That was a nuisance. Anyway Mummu took a lamp and spent the night chasing off the dogs that were prowling and fighting some way off. At midnight the sky grew black and dark. Though he was inside the shop, tea-shop owner Mummu was scared.

After a while a gale began to blow and heavy rain to fall. Mummu saw this as a piece of good fortune. When morning came the body was all bloated up and decomposition had set in; but all the excreta and vomit had mixed with the water and had been washed, by the way of the place where people went to bathe, into the canal. The spot where the corpse lay in front of Mummu's tea-shop was now clean.

As the day wore on, the stench increased! By noon it was unbearable. That day things did not go so well for Mummu. There were practically no cash sales. Only the credit customers from among the employees of the Spinwell Company showed up.

Once again the shopkeepers in the immediate vicinity all put their heads together to find a solution. There was still no sign of anyone coming. What about the stench? It was unbearable. Someone went to fetch the lawyer's clerk. His view, after he had given the matter careful thought, was that they should send a petition signed by all who lived close by.

It was agreed. Straight away pen and paper were brought. The lawyer's clerk went on: 'There shouldn't be any loopholes. Give it a bit of thought and then write it.'

As the lawyer's clerk began to draft the petition, the boy who worked in the tea-shop ran up to say that people had come from the municipality. It seemed that Mummu was wanted there right away.

There was a refuse cart, and three or four scavengers were there, along with Joseph, the overseer. The overseer was in the process of writing something with great seriousness. The tea-shop owner greeted the overseer in a most obsequious fashion.

Lifting his head, the overseer asked, 'Who is it lying dead there?'

Mummu shook with fear. 'I don't know!'

'When did this man die?'

'Yesterday morning I saw him lying there already dead.'

'Who gave you permission to do business while leaving this corpse lying here like this?'

Mummu had no reply to that question. He was at fault. Mummu had not anticipated such a question. The overseer took an even sterner tone. 'Why are you standing there with nothing to say?'

'It – it – Sir, please save me, please, I beg you.'

Grinding his teeth, the overseer looked Mummu up and down. Once again he began writing. By that time the lawyer's clerk was there too. The clerk, an extremely astute fellow, went up to the overseer.

The two of them moved away a little to talk. Mummu, the tobacco-seller Kittan and the lawyer's clerk all had another consultation. And from the lawyer's clerk's hand a small packet containing money fell into the overseer's pocket.

Without any lessening of his former seriousness, the overseer looked at Mummu. Pointing at the lawyer's clerk, he said, 'Because of him I'm letting you off this time.'

Mummu bowed low in gratitude. The lawyer's clerk seemed to grow taller with pride.

The scavengers lifted the body on to the cart. Are they not human beings? Yet do they not have to perform such tasks as picking up and handling this rotting corpse? The overseer told Mummu that he should at least have the generosity to give them something to drink. Anything would do. Gladly Mummu went along with that too.

Cholera!

It is not possible to estimate the number of deaths in the town of Alleppey during that outbreak. This is because the people who die are not included as part of the population of human beings. They are beggars, poor people and suchlike. They are to be seen being picked up, one after the other, from roadsides and street corners.

How can one keep count! It is an impossibility. Moreover, do any of these dying creatures even have a name?

Later it was rumoured that some from among the better class of people had died. It was possible that the municipality might be informed of some of these deaths. So the town of Alleppey spent its days unpleasantly and fearfully in the black shadow of death.

Where was salvation to be found? What was the nature of that salvation? Who would be saved? No one knew when they would be struck down. In the twinkling of an eye, life became uncertain and the future dark and dreadful.

Does one not need something to hold on to, for comfort? Is it not necessary to have faith that one can escape such a plague? One may inevitably catch it. But if, until one's last breath, one has faith that one will be saved, the agony of death is reduced.

On occasions like this certain beliefs handed down through generations will sustain you. The goddess of cholera and smallpox is Kali. In Mullaikkal the offering of flowers, the worship of the goddess, the sprinkling of holy water began. St George it was who slew the devil. Once again in Alleppey they began to make offerings to him.

Even then it was business as usual in the tea-shops; people bathed in the Wada Stream and in the Commercial Canal. Life flowed on unhindered. The only sign was that people one saw yesterday were not to be seen today.

If one wished to see the true shape of the fearful dance of death, the place to go was the burial ground. Every day at daybreak numerous long heaps of sand could be seen rising up there; funeral pyres that had burnt and subsided. The cemeteries, lit up by the flames of the pyres, were alive at night-time with the shouting of scavengers who had drunk themselves almost senseless on toddy.

After a few days dogs began to dig and pull out the dead bodies. Every day eight or ten bodies were uncovered. Apparently there were even the bodies of shopkeepers and officials among them!

Then the matter became serious. The news came out that the bodies in the cemetery were not buried deep enough. It was decided in the town council that someone should be appointed to watch over the burial ground.

The creation of the new post was to Chudalamuttu's advantage. It was he who became the first cemetery watchman.

They had stipulated how the cemetery watchman should be dressed: black shorts, black shirt and a long stick. So that was how Chudalamuttu took his place on a high spot at the entrance to the cemetery. On his stick was a mark showing the depth of a grave.

In that way Chudalamuttu gave up the shovel and bucket entrusted to him by his father. He would not take them up again. That was all he wanted. Chudalamuttu was no longer a scavenger. Nor was his son a scavenger's son.

When he went and stood at the cemetery gateway with his long stick and his black attire Chudalamuttu had prepared a plan relating to the new job. He knew what authority he had; he knew what he was able to do.

When the black figure took his position at the entrance to that enclosure where life ends, it seemed as if the fearfulness of the place increased. Before life was over, you now had to account to one more person. The scavenger, who until a day ago was working in your latrine, when he came to his new place he was a different person. Looking at him, passers-by said, 'Look, is it death's messenger who is standing there?'

They took people through that gate to give them the six feet of ground that each individual is entitled to. No matter who it was, it was Chudalamuttu who decided on the spot. When the grave was dug Chudalamuttu would take his measuring stick to see if it was deep enough. Only after getting permission from him could they fill it in. If someone was to be cremated he had the authority to refuse to allow it on the grounds of insufficient firewood. Within two days Chudalamuttu had learnt how much firewood was needed for one person.

Nevertheless it was not possible for Chudalamuttu to do his job there unemotionally. He would often see them burning the bones of young children. He would watch them burying those who had died at a tender age. How long the bones of very old men smoulder! If they are to die so young, thought Chudalamuttu, why were they born? Has that young man done all that he was born to do? And that old man, why had he lived so long? If it comes to that, at what age should a person die? At forty? Fifty? Sixty? . . . If at fifty, Chudalamuttu would calculate, then how many years did he have left? How many years had Valli ahead of her? And how many had Mohanan?

Burnt pieces of bone lay scattered here and there in the graveyard. Whose bones were they? Sometimes, when they dug a grave, skulls and ribcages – of different ages – were fetched up. How many people were buried there, along with all their hopes and aspirations!

On some nights, with everyone gone, the cemetery would be deserted. From the still-burning pyre, a dim light would be given out. Then Chudalamuttu would be afraid. But he did not have to sit a long time alone like that. For it was cholera time, was it not? And in the night the shrouded bodies kept on coming.

One night one of the bodies covered in this way was Muniswami's . . . Another night it was Palaniyandi and his two children. Thus death began to take its share from the scavenger colony too. In the course of a week many of Chudalamuttu's acquaintances died and were brought to the graveyard. And not only scavengers, but also several people from the houses where he had worked.

This extended activity of death, this direct transaction with dying, shook both the mind and the courage of Chudalamuttu. The illiterate scavenger – who people considered to be lacking in imagination – was able, albeit vaguely, to see something of the world and of life beyond his own nose. He realised that there was no certainty in life. Turning around without a sure foothold, without anything they can even grip firmly, living beings drift along, caught in this powerful current. He too was drifting with the rest; so too were his Valli and Mohanan. Who knew whether he, and she, and his dear son would be alive tomorrow?

Chudalamuttu became frightened. Where was there to hide? When he left the house Chudalamuttu was anxious about what was happening there. Every minute he was expecting sad news.

What if they were to go away from this town and from the area affected by the plague? Never mind about the house and compound. He spoke to Valli about it.

'It's not good to stay here. All our lot are dying off. Let's go.'

She had suggested that long ago. Now that her husband was of the same opinion she was relieved.

How frightened Chudalamuttu became! He was afraid that he would fall down dead the next minute, that an end like that had been decreed. When plagues like this had executed their dance before in the town Valli had seen Chudalamuttu stand unshaken. She wondered what the reason was now for this powerful fear. She tried to console her husband: 'All of this is fate. What has to be will be. If it's the will of God, we can't prevent it. What good will it do if you are scared like this?'

Yet Valli's equanimity was also shaken. Even her belief in fate could not give her much assurance. But she had a duty as a wife to give comfort to her husband and she had the self-confidence to do it, at least in name.

'Among our lot, who is still alive?' she asked.

'I don't know, I don't know. They're all finished, all of them. No work's being done in the municipality.'

After a short while Valli continued her words of consolation: 'Though you once said that I don't think about God, I now say my prayers and put garlands on the deity's picture. In the evening I sprinkle water there and light the lamp. At times like these, having faith in God is the only way to escape.'

She did not feel that what she said made any impression on Chudalamuttu. Though he heard it, he did not understand. He believed that nothing could save them. A disaster was unavoidable; it was imminent. But he had no idea what form it would take.

'Why don't you pray these days?' Valli asked.

'It just hasn't been possible.'

'Even though you're in the cemetery, can't you pray in the evening? There's no rule that you can only pray in certain places.'

He promised to pray from then on. He would continue in the old ways. Though he spoke in these terms, inside Chudalamuttu the anxieties were straining to get out. They filled him to overflowing. All this time he had borne their pain alone. Why, he thought, should he tell her and trouble her with them too? But now he could no longer bear it alone and he said, 'Valli! That's not what I'm thinking. It's true we should have faith in God. In God Almighty is salvation. It's not that . . .' Chudalamuttu stammered; there were tears in his eyes.

'We have no close relatives. We are alone. Is there anyone who loves us? For me there is you, and for you me. And for our child, us.'

Valli's eyes, too, filled with tears. In this wide world they were alone – completely alone! For a moment Pichandi's form passed like a shadow through Chudalamuttu's mind and disappeared. He trembled. He was unable to think straight. Tears streamed from his eyes. Valli, too, wept. She went up to her husband and wiped his tears.

'What foolishness is this?'

That was all she could say. Overwhelmed with sadness, Chudalamuttu asked, 'No – if I die – what will the two of you do?'

Valli was taken aback: 'What madness is this?'

'It's not madness. All those who are dead are brought there. Those ghosts – those ghosts . . .'

Chudalamuttu was afraid. He was afraid as if he saw those spirits of the dead before him. Valli was frightened. She threw her arms round her husband.

'What is all this?'

'Oh, it's nothing, nothing. No, Valli! My dear Valli! You have looked after me for so long. You are a good person. All I ask is that you look after my son. Please take care of him.'

Chudalamuttu was utterly convinced that he would fall victim to the plague.

'That won't happen. God won't allow it to happen. When I die, you bury me – but please look after my son. Even if I die he will grow up.'

'But what if his father dies?'

This is a conversation that will only be heard in a place where the wife loves the husband and the husband loves the wife. The wife wishing to close her eyes in death only after seeing her husband again and again and entrusting her children to the security of her husband's strong arms; the husband wishing to die with his chest cooled by her tears. Is this not something that is found everywhere? But it remained to be seen whose wish would be granted.

Chudalamuttu's thoughts had taken another direction: 'What if we both die?'

The child! Their child! Whom does he have but them? In a moment Chudalamuttu saw a crowd of children, orphaned through the death of their fathers and mothers, appearing one by one in all corners of the town. Among them were Sundiran's children!

'God will not let anything like that happen.'

Like one who was out of his mind, Chudalamuttu held Valli's hand tightly and said, 'Let's go, Valli! Let's go away from this place.'

Chudalamuttu's grip relaxed. Another fact to be faced! He saw the president; he asked for the money. The president said he did not have the money in ready cash at the moment.

'We don't want the money. We don't want anything. Let's leave with our lives.'

'Then – then – let's go.'

'But supposing we go? How shall we live?'

How was she to console him? What reply was she to give?

Valli bathed Mohanan, her son, put the customary mark on his forehead, dressed him in clean shorts and shirt, committed him to the care of God, gave him a kiss and sent him to school. She watched him till he disappeared from sight. Dear child! Whom did he have but them? Tears came to Valli's eyes.

Mohanan was constantly looking back. When Valli went back into the house he stopped. His playmate, the beggar boy, shot up from behind and said, 'When I saw your mother standing there I kept out of sight.'

Mohanan answered, 'I saw you too.'

The two of them were pleased with themselves for meeting without Valli knowing. That day Mohanan had a couple of chakrams on him. The beggar boy had managed to get three chakrams. He intended to get another ten chakrams in the course of the day.

'Today there's a big festival in Mullaikkal. By big festival, I mean a *big* festival. From the time it gets dark there'll be fireworks. There are ten elephants. Today is the best of all. I've just come from there.' And he began to describe how the place was decorated.

'Will you take me to have a look too?' asked Mohanan.

'Why not? If you come now we can soon run there. We'll see it and then come back.'

'I'm supposed to be at school.'

'Oh! A school's just a school. We can go and return without your mother seeing.'

His youthful conscience was facing a crisis. He had never failed to turn up at school.

The boy asked something else: 'Won't the schoolmaster beat you?'

'Yes. He does so every day. He's that sort of teacher.'

Then Mohanan remembered something else. He had not done the homework he should have had ready for that day. He had forgotten. So his next question was, 'Where shall I put this slate and book?'

His pal said that was no problem. They turned off from that road into another. The beggar boy, who was familiar with the area, took Mohanan's books and left them for safe-keeping in a shop at the corner.

So many new sights, so many new places! Drinking it all in, Mohanan went along with him till they reached Mullaikkal.

Everything he had said was true. What decorations! They were really worth going to see. For Mohanan it was a completely new world.

That was the day when ten elephants could be seen together. In one place there was a magic show; in another a game played with small sticks; in yet another a gymnastic display. Thus he went along seeing the various sights. They had a couple of rides on the big wheel. At one place, where they paid two chakrams to go in, they saw a spider talking. Further on were the puppets which danced, jumped and spoke.

In that way all their money got used up. It was noon, and there were still many things left to do. The boy said he would soon be back, after he had been to make some more money. He put Mohanan on the platform under a banyan tree and went off, having instructed him not to go anywhere. If he were to go, it would be difficult to find him. Then the boy disappeared in the crowd.

Mohanan began to feel afraid. He was alone! There was not a familiar face in sight. He thought of his mother; of his father; he could not stop himself from crying. He could not bear his hunger. So the child, whose father and mother had always treasured him like gold, grew tired and faint and fell asleep there on the platform.

The boy returned and poked him to wake him up. Then he asked, 'Do you want to eat something?'

'Yes.'

'Then come along. I've had a meal.'

Beckoning Mohanan, he went to a hotel. Mohanan ate his fill. What tasty curry!

When he had finished eating, the other boy took out a couple of chakrams from his pocket to pay for it. He still had some chakrams left. And not only chakrams, but annas and fanams too! Where did he get so much money? Mohanan thought how good it would be if he could get money like that. So they walked on, seeing all the fun and buying sweets and cashew-nuts to eat. In the midst of all the sights Mohanan quite forgot his mother and father and his home. He just went along taking it all in.

Four o'clock came, then five, then six. They were bringing something in a procession for the Shribali ceremony. A drummer from Pondicherry was beating his drum, and it was fun to see how his hair became dishevelled and waved about. He made such funny faces! In another spot a score of large drums were being beaten at the same time. One man was blowing a pipe that was bent like a bow.

The whole place was decorated, and when he saw all the coloured lights burning together Mohanan thought it was really great. Then it was time for the fireworks. The first few times he heard the explosions he was scared. Later, when the bangers and rockets went off, he too made a noise along with them.

At night they had a meal; they also had a snack in a tea-shop. Mohanan bought a balloon and a whistle too.

So, worn out with all the walking, Mohanan and the boy got as far as the wall on the northern side of the Brahmin eating-house in Mullaikkal. Even as they were talking, they fell asleep.

When it was well and truly daylight Mohanan woke up. Where had he lain down to sleep? Mother! Mother! Father!

With his shirt and shorts covered in dirt, and feeling very frightened, Mohanan went and stood by the door of his home and peeped in. The beggar boy stood a little further away, to find out whether Mohanan's mother would beat him. If there was going to be a beating then he wanted to see it.

For a while Mohanan stood on the threshold. The door was open. There was nobody to be seen. He thought his mother might be in the kitchen. But there was no smoke coming from that direction.

Filled with guilt, his heart beating fast, the lad stood there for some time. A goat had got into the yard and was eating the holy basil that had been planted there. His mother used to pick it for use in her *pooja*. Mohanan drove the goat away. Even though this made a noise, his mother did not come out.

He thought he heard someone snoring inside the house. Though the day was so far advanced, perhaps his mother had not yet got up. Maybe she had spent the whole of the previous day walking all over Mullaikkal in search of him and had come back and slept.

Slowly Mohanan peeped into the kitchen. All the pots and pans there were overturned. They had not even been scoured. There was no sign of the stove having been lit even on the previous day.

Mohanan peeped inside the house. Valli was lying on her back in a mixture of excreta and vomit. It was when she breathed in and out that a sound like that of snoring could be heard. Her belly was bloated up so that it was higher than her chest.

Mohanan stood for a moment in the doorway and then went inside. Even then, with his feeling of guilt, the boy was afraid that, when his mother opened her eyes and saw him, she would scold and beat him.

When he had stood in the room for a short while, he became frightened. His mother was not sleeping; nor was she really breathing. His fear that she would beat him left him. He called out, 'Mother!'

His mother did not respond.

He was afraid to go near her; he was afraid to stand and look.

The whole of Valli's body shook. Her eyes were open. Mohanan shuddered.

All was silent and still!

He felt it was not his mother. His mother's eyes were not like that; her mouth would not be wide open in that way. It was someone else. A devil! A ghost!

The beggar boy had now come right inside. He, too, had seen it all. He took hold of Mohanan and ran outside, dragging him along. He understood what it all meant.

At noon the previous day the cemetery watchman had shown signs of cholera. When day dawned, he was to be seen lying dead in the place where he usually stood.

Mohanan, along with the boy, went to the cemetery. Another man was using Chudalamuttu's stick to measure the depth of a large grave. Near the grave was a body, wrapped round and tied, but with the head and feet still visible.

Mohanan realised that it was his father.

Those two boys are now to be seen, their arms round each other, lying asleep in the dust on the edge of the road near the boat jetty . . . Sometimes Mohanan fights with other children. He does not know how to use his fists. As a result he is the one who gets most beatings . . . At other times the one playing the game of diving deep down in the Wada Stream or the Commercial Canal like an otter is Mohanan. Those souls filled with parental love that hover around him in the sky must become afraid when he goes down . . . No doubt they wipe the dust from his body when he gets up from sleeping in the roadside dirt. Is there any other deity that would save him from the many perils of this sort of existence?

Mohanan – why did they give him that name? When lawyer Kurup's wife had burst out laughing, it had not been a meaning-less laugh. It was for his sake that two living beings had given up all thoughts of a comfortable life.

'For ten days only can we enjoy life.'

For ten days alone they had enjoyed it. Where is the house and compound that Chudalamuttu dreamt of? Where is the money he entrusted to the president?

Pichandi's and Sundiran's children on either side, and Mohanan in the middle, have thus embarked on life's journey at a tender age. He now gets his food from the waste-bins of hotels.

Vengeance

A few years passed. The husband who had wished to die in the comfort of being cared for by his wife, the wife who had wished to die gazing at her husband; both died without their prayers being answered. Could it be that Valli lost consciousness before there was time for her to be anxious about her son's failure to come back from school? She had not been able to entrust her son to the care of her husband. Could she have known about it, when Mohanan came and called her the next morning? Her eyes had become fixed before she breathed her last. Did she see him then? However it may have been, she would not have known either that her husband had died or that her son went around with street urchins.

What about the cemetery watchman? He, too, had a consolation. His wife would take care of his child. At the same time, had he seen them both, he would not have failed to ask a few things of her. He had not had a chance to give his son his last blessing. He must also have had some advice to give.

So the couple that passed away had changed into earth, water, air and fire. The grass that grew over them had been sprouting afresh each rainy season after being burnt off by the sun. Is it possible to be sure that, unknown to anyone, the long roots of some huge tree standing some way off or of a shrub growing inside the enclosure have not penetrated into the graves? Will not their bones have crumbled and turned into dust?

Yet something of those parents went on existing that neither wind, nor rain, nor summer sun, nor time could destroy. Is not the eternal soul in us, that the religious proclaim, a manifestation of God's presence? Not only that; whether we walk, or sit, or lie down, do we not experience fearful unease, anxiety about the future and a feeling of indecision? Has life not come to mean overcoming the difficulties that oppress the mind? Has modern life not reached a state of uncertainty? Today everyone says it is not worth living. Man fears life. When one thinks how this destructive sadness was brought into being, one can explain what is left of Chudalamuttu and Valli. Turn your gaze backwards. How many millions of Chudalamuttus and Vallis have been ground down and destroyed like this! For how many years has this been going on! Where else could all their desires and dreams, their love and hate, be absorbed except in this atmosphere? If the air you breathe has become heavier, is this to be wondered at? If you feel that the ground beneath your feet is not firm, if your foothold is unsteady, there is a reason for it. Blood lies congealed in that ground. If you feel you have enemies all around, remember for how many centuries you have been making enemies.

So the spirits of that couple played their part in increasing the uneasiness of life in Alleppey town. Before this, how many thousands of dead scavengers' and sweepers' desires, dreams and anger had added to the heaviness of the atmosphere?

Chudalamuttu hoped that his son would not become a scavenger. He gave him a name that did not go with being a scavenger. The boy grew up ignorant of the meaning of the word 'scavenger'. The father used to be furious if he saw his child lying in dirt for even a short while. But today that child is a scavenger in Alleppey town. His superiors raise their eyebrows when they learn that his name is Mohanan!

'Hm, the scavenger, too, is coming up in the world.'

Pichandi's son and Sundiran's son are now scavengers along with him. The three of them are joined together in kinship, like soldiers fighting against the same enemy.

Like his father, Mohanan goes every morning with bucket and shovel into each latrine. When his bucket is full he transfers it into drums that have been placed on the roadside. At ten o'clock he must help to lift those drums on to the night-soil lorry that comes that way. In the evening he is to be seen along with his friends, in the park or on the beach, clean and well-dressed.

Today's scavenger knows how much he earns; he has also learnt to get change for his money without being cheated. He even has the nerve to want higher wages. In Alleppey the scavengers have learnt to speak with a united voice.

They have a well-organised union which has accomplished many things. They realise it could achieve much.

Mohanan is not married. Nor are his friends. Not that they have not thought of marriage. They talk about it once in a while. Mohanan is not afraid of the possibility that, if there are any children, they will become scavengers. He knows that it is not scavengers who create scavengers. It just so happens that there are scavengers. Even if a father thinks his child should not become a scavenger, that child might become one.

There is a widespread complaint that scavengers are insolent. If you try to investigate that complaint you will hear that they are indeed insolent. They have been cleaning the latrines; they have been coming on time. But . . . but . . . you should see the way he walks in the evening! He uses talcum powder; he wears a *jubba*; he smokes cigarettes. He is not subservient.

That is true. The Alleppey scavenger has learnt quite a bit. He knows quite a bit. He knows how to think on the basis of what he knows and thus get to know more. So he behaves as one lost in thought. He has realised that a scavenger is a human being.

The Municipal Workers' Union has submitted a plan for town development to the municipal council and to the government. It has come to that – the scavengers have something to say! Both the government and the municipality have cautioned the union. The union has no right to interfere in these things. The union is an association for furthering the interests of the municipal workers. What they are now concerning themselves with has political implications. They should not meddle in it.

That day Mohanan said to his friends, 'Now do you understand what I said long ago? What is it that we have to stand against? Is it this municipality? In reality it is not the individual boss who is the worker's enemy. It is the boss's government.'

A scavenger's son also has memories. Just as a prince's son can remember his father and mother, so a scavenger's son can remember his. Perhaps, when that fortunate prince speaks of his parents, he might be able to see only just as much as is necessary to say, 'They loved me.' For the infant of such wealthy parents will not be brought up breast-fed by his mother. If he becomes ill, the mother need not lose sleep for long. When they look about them, there is no need for much anxiety about the child's future.

Millions of Mohanans have blurred recollections engraved on their minds of all the Chudalamuttus and Vallis who lived in suffering and privation for the sake of their children. Occasionally, from those unclear memories, there will emerge an anger so intense that it can burn the whole world to ashes. Thinking about it all at other times, he will sit there weak and helpless, and cry. On other occasions still, an unclear message will, with its destructive force, make him go mad. He is the living embodiment of the power of his ancestor's vengeance that was thought to have been suppressed.

It was on the day that Pichandi's son became a scavenger that he got a name. Sundiran's son has a recollection of being given some name. He remembers his mother being carried away. He thinks she called out to her children. Anyway, when Dad called, Mother replied, 'Husband.' That reply still resounds in his ears. Apparently he had an elder sister and a younger brother . . . When he woke up one morning he was all alone. He does not know where the others are! He never saw them again. Today he is still searching for his lost brother and sister.

In the midst of a heated argument in the union office, or whenever he is walking alone along the beach or when he goes with his bucket to work, Mohanan also thinks. It is those memories that keep him going. His father and mother ended their lives crushed beneath the weight of this big city. He knows they wanted him to become somebody. His mother would place him on her lap, his father would sit nearby and the two would talk about something. They sent him to school. His schooling was the most important thing in their lives. Though his father did not pick him up or kiss him, yet he was the personification of paternal affection . . . What prayers he used to say as a boy! All his mother prayed for was for him. They had money. Yes; he had heard his father working it out . . . That amount was with the president . . .

What an enormously wealthy man the president was! All the important buildings in the town were his. Mohanan felt he had a right to all this property. His father's life-blood was included in that wealth.

Once in a while he would see the president going by in a motor car. And often he would think: supposing he were to go and ask for the money? Would he still remember Chudalamuttu the scavenger? How many Chudalamuttus had he killed and buried? . . . Who in that town remembered Chudalamuttu?

This scavenger's emotions have blossomed and taken on a shape that is as yet ill-defined. He has started dreaming about the blaze of fire rising into the sky and about the spilling of blood. He does not know what the fire will feed on, nor from whose chest the blood will gush out.

One day there took place the inauguration of a huge mansion built by that old municipal president. It was a special event. There was no building in town as large as that one. Mohanan and his friends stood and watched.

That day Mohanan did not get to sleep till midnight. He was jerked out of the light sleep that followed by a dream . . . That big mansion had caught fire and the flames were rising high into the sky!

Mohanan's dreams took on a definite shape.

His friends advised him: 'Why do you feel this way, Mohanan? This will defeat our objectives. The wrongs they have done to us are in no way less than those they have done to you.'

Mohanan said, 'I just want to know what the sum of money was that my father entrusted to him for me.'

'Sum of money!' Pichandi's son laughed. Sum of money! How many sums scavengers have lost! All the children of scavengers are asking for accounts.

Mohanan was not convinced; he did not feel satisfied. He would not rest without revenge. Sundiran's son looked at his face and said harshly, 'Your father's desire to become a man of wealth and position is mixed with your blood too. The desire for revenge stems from that.'

'Maybe you're right,' Mohanan agreed. If not, why should he want to know what his father's savings came to? His wish was still for individual ownership.

Pichandi's son said, 'We should forget the individual and oppose the state of society that that individual represents. In that opposition the target of your revenge will also be destroyed.'

None of this seemed to get through to Mohanan. The blaze of fire and the spilling of blood were becoming clearer in his mind's eye every minute. Now he must see these sights with his real eyes. That was the only way out.

Pichandi's son continued: 'Anyhow, we shall always be behind you in everything.'

The town grew black and dark. Life became anxious. No one knew what would happen from one minute to the next. The volcano was smoking. No one knew when it would erupt.

The poor worker who lives starving and deprived in the low huts that are to be seen around us – him we do not fear. What can he do to us? Are we afraid of the beggar who comes, leaning on a crude stick, and stands at our door calling out for alms? Till today, has the low-caste worker who toils in the fields beneath the rain and the hot sun ever stood up against anybody? . . . But today we are afraid, not of those individuals, but of the sum total of their emotions. With every day, every minute, it is taking on gigantic proportions.

Is the fear only because of that? Is there not a sense of guilt for the wrongs we have done?

General strike! In the name of public order the army was streaming into the town.

The town had come to a complete standstill. There was no activity of any sort. The streets were deserted.

So one day passed. Curled up in the womb of that silence there lay a hurricane. It was not possible for that huge thing to remain still and quiet like that and not have an effect. The explosion was inevitable. The town was aware of that. The next day there was a huge workers' demonstration; not only in the town, but in the surrounding parts too.

As the demonstration might be the cause of a breach of the peace, the authorities issued a warning beforehand that it would be stopped. But that only served to increase the workers' strength. There was opposition; their emotions were sharpened.

*   *   *

The expected happened. The chain of events resulted in confusion. Crowds of people came in their thousands and formed processions in many places. The demonstration was meant to be entirely peaceful. But the size of the section of the populace who had experienced nothing but privation and sorrow, half naked and half starving as they were, frightened not just the town, but the whole state. It included not only the workers, but also beggars, lepers and so on! Were there this many people asking for their rights? In the enjoyment of their own good fortune, no one had realised that the size of this class was so big.

Almost all of them are our neighbours; they are people we are closely associated with; people who show respect when they stand before us; people who live in a state of dependence on us. Not one of them is a person we fear . . . Yet if we see him, as he stands there with his belly almost touching his back and wearing nothing but a *dhoti*, roaring and rushing forward, we are afraid. His eyes roll. Where were this strength and this anger hidden?

He is saying they will take their rights by force! Moreover, he has the ability to do this.

The army stood in the path of all the processions. The answer to zeal was the aiming of rifles. The shots were not able to break the line.

So shooting and processions continued for several days. There was no destruction of property in the town. But there was fear! In spite of the stationing of a very strong army detachment in the town, there was uncontrollable fear.

This fear is not one that can be controlled because it is not a fear born of external power, which will end when that power is destroyed. It is a fear that each person has created within his own heart; it is the fruit of each one's actions. It was born centuries ago and is still growing. Will there ever be a time when human beings can live without fear?

The demonstrators had strict instructions that there must be no violence. This was to be just a demonstration of the poor man's strength. Those instructions, despite continuous shooting and provocation, were obeyed for almost a week. Nowhere was there any use of force from the side of the demonstrators.

*   *   *

In the scavenger colony Pichandi's son and Sundiran's son were sitting together indoors beside a lamp. Pichandi's son said softly, 'It's so late and still he's not here. Where can he have got to?'

Sundiran's son replied, 'Has he met with an accident?'

Then someone was heard knocking at the door. Pichandi's son jumped up and opened it. Mohanan came in.

He was out of breath and sweating profusely. And what an agitated look there was on his face! But it did not seem to be caused by fear. Pichandi's son asked him: 'What is it, Mohanan?'

He could not tell them. He pointed outside through the open window. There in the distance they saw flames dancing. They understood. It was the new building belonging to the municipal president.

With his hand on his chest, Pichandi's son said, 'You have betrayed us.'

Mohanan was enjoying watching the flames. Finally, when there was nothing left but a glow, he was able to speak and he said calmly, 'Yes, I betrayed you; it's true. This is a breach of discipline. Due to me our undertaking has received a hard blow. But I am a man. Should not my dreams be realised?' His friends saw his relief.

The next day it was he who led the procession through the important parts of the town. The participants were lined up one behind the other in two ranks. In front stood Mohanan carrying a large flag.

'Long live the revolution!'

'The revolution!' That cry broke the walls of the heavens.

With tears in their eyes, Pichandi's son and Sundiran's son each put a red garland on him.

They began singing a battle song that would give them renewed energy. Keeping in step with the rhythm, the procession moved off.

His flag was fluttering in the breeze. The crowd, unarmed and possessing only spiritual strength, moved forward under the leadership of the scavenger's son. His face bore the serious and resolute expression befitting a leader.

*   *   *

By the time it reached the other side of town that huge procession
had been reduced by three-quarters . . . Comrades had been shot
down at three paces. Nevertheless the shots did not succeed in
dispersing it. Without a single empty space, and with the line
unbroken, the procession moved on.

On some waste land away from the town can be seen a large
mound. Day by day the ground has settled and it has become
smaller and smaller. Some years have passed. When the sand was
washed away a few skeletons could be clearly seen on the mound.
On the neck of one skeleton a few red threads were visible.

Some say that today, on that waste land, the skeletons dance!

Glossary

beedi   a cheap cigarette made of fragments of tobacco wrapped in a leaf

coir   coarse fibre from the husk of a coconut, used for making ropes, matting, etc.

dhobi   washerman

dhoti   man's lower garment, consisting of a length of cloth

dosha   a type of pancake made from rice flour

Durga pooja   worship of the Hindu goddess Durga. Durga is one of the names of the wife of Siva. She is a goddess of great power; the divine protectress, who slays evil like the demon buffalo

jubba   long outer garment with long sleeves, worn normally by officials and professional men.

kanji   rice boiled in a large amount of water until it becomes soft; a kind of gruel

payasam   a liquid milk-based sweet dish

pooja   Hindu act of worship

sanyasi   a Hindu religious ascetic

tali   a thread, of gold where possible, tied round an Indian bride's neck by the bridegroom at the marriage ceremony